BEWARE!!
DO NOT READ THIS
BOOK FROM
BEGINNING TO END!

You wake up with a jolt. What a scary nightmare! You were trapped in a strange place — you were being chased — and you had no idea who you were! You sure are glad that's over.

But as you stretch and look around, you realize you are in a strange place — and you can't remember your own name! There's a loud banging on the door. Who is it? A friend or an enemy? Do you tell whoever is behind the door your story? Or hide and hope they go away? One thing is for sure. You have to find out who you are, and how to get home — fast.

This strange, scary adventure is all about you. You decide what will happen. And you decide how terrifying the scares will be!

Start on *PAGE 1*. Then follow the instructions at the bottom of each page. You make the choices. If you choose well, you'll make it home again. But if you make the wrong choice . . . BEWARE!

SO TAKE A DEEP BREATH, CROSS YOUR FINGERS, AND TURN TO *PAGE 1* TO *GIVE YOURSELF GOOSEBUMPS*!

READER BEWARE —
YOU CHOOSE THE SCARE!

Look for more
GIVE YOURSELF GOOSEBUMPS adventures
from R.L. STINE:

R.L. STINE

GIVE YOURSELF

Goosebumps®

ALL-DAY NIGHTMARE

AN
APPLE
PAPERBACK

SCHOLASTIC INC.
New York Toronto London Auckland
Sydney New Delhi Hong Kong

A PARACHUTE PRESS BOOK

ISBN-13: 978-0-439-13530-6

This edition is for sale in Indian subcontinent only.
First Scholastic printing, February 2000

Reprinted by Scholastic India Pvt. Ltd., January; March 2008
January; August 2010, November 2011; July; August;
December 2013; August; December 2014

Printed at Shivam Offset Press, New Delhi

"Ahhhhhh!" you scream.

And then you wake up.

Whoa! you think, shaking your head. That was some nightmare. You're soaked in sweat. Your heart is pounding like crazy.

Horrible images from the dream still dance in your mind. You remember two-foot-tall creatures chasing you. They had long arms that scraped against the floor as they ran.

Creepy.

You also remember a huge spinning wheel of fire. And a terrible screeching sound, louder than a jet engine.

What a weird dream!

At least it's over. You're glad to be back in your nice warm bed.

Only, your bed *isn't* very warm. And it's pretty hard too.

Hey. Wait a minute.

You're on the floor!

Oh, brother! you think. You must have rolled out of bed. Well, it's time to get back to sleep. You stand up, looking around your room.

But it's *not* your room!

Where *are* you?

Turn to PAGE 2.

2

What's going on here?

Even in the dark, you know that you've never been in this place before. You stumble around the room, crashing into unfamiliar furniture. Finally you find a light switch.

CLICK. Nothing. No electricity.

A cold sweat starts to run down your back.

The room smells dusty and unused. Like no one's lived here for a hundred years. You feel yourself starting to panic.

How did you get here?

Calm down, you order yourself. There must be a logical explanation for this.

You try to remember where you went to sleep. Were you staying over at a friend's house? Visiting Grandma? At summer camp?

That's funny, you think. You can't remember a thing!

But you know you're not supposed to be *here.* That's as sure as your name is . . .

. . . is . . . ?

Uh-oh.

You can't remember your name!

Turn to PAGE 3.

Who *are* you?

Your head falls into your hands. You wrack your brain, trying to remember something . . . *anything*! But your memory is totally gone.

Where do you live? What do your parents look like? How old are you?

You just don't know.

Do you have any brothers or sisters? What school do you go to? What *happened* to you?

This is too weird.

Okay, you tell yourself. It's time to calm down. You can't figure this out by panicking!

You stride to the door and open it. You're facing a long hallway lined with doors. The doors are crooked and warped with age. The hallway floor seems slanted. The whole thing makes you dizzy, like a hall of mirrors.

Then a chill runs up your spine. You've seen this hallway before! Was it in your dream?

You take a nervous step forward.

Suddenly, a door in the hallway opens.

"Who are you?" a voice demands.

Go to PAGE 4.

4

You peer into the darkness. You can just make out a boy your age staring warily back at you.

"Uh — I —" you stammer. "I don't know who I am!"

You gulp. He must think you're nuts! But he nods his head.

"You too?" he asks. "I can't remember who I am, either. I just woke up, and I don't have a clue how I got here."

You scrutinize the boy. He's tall and has dark hair. He's wearing a T-shirt that says TO THE MAX.

"Look at your shirt," you say. "Maybe your name is Max!"

He stares down at the shirt and frowns. "I have no idea," he says. You decide to call him Max, anyway. You've got to call him *something*.

"All I remember is this crazy nightmare," Max continues.

Your jaw drops. "Nightmare?"

The boy squints, thinking hard. "Yeah. There were these little people, about two feet tall."

"With long arms?" you ask. Eyes wide, he nods his head.

"And a wheel of fire," you continue. "And a terrible screeching noise."

A look of horror fills his face. "We had the same dream!"

"Maybe it wasn't a dream —" you begin.

"Shhh!" he interrupts. "Did you hear that?"

Go to PAGE 5.

You clamp your mouth shut and listen.

It sounds like someone is banging on a door below you. You must be on the second floor of this house.

A nervous trickle of sweat runs down your back.

"Who do you think is down there?" you whisper.

"How should I know?" Max mutters.

The banging comes again, making you jump.

"Listen," you command. "Maybe we both got knocked on the head and lost our memory. And whoever's down there is looking for us."

"Yeah, maybe," Max answers. "Of course, maybe *they* knocked us on the head! Something pretty weird has happened to us. Maybe we should hide. At least until we know what's going on."

What should you do? Go downstairs and say hi? Or stay hidden?

To answer the door, turn to PAGE 34.
To stay hidden, turn to PAGE 98.

6

"Downstairs!" you order Max. You've got to get out of this house! You thunder down the stairs together.

At the bottom, you find yourself in an old kitchen. An ancient stove squats in one corner. A dusty table sits next to one wall.

"Look! The back door!" shouts Max.

You both run toward the back door. You grasp the handle and pull.

Oh, no! It's locked!

You smash your shoulder into it. But it doesn't open.

Overhead, you hear the dogs barking.

"Together!" Max commands.

You lower your shoulder and barrel into the back door. It crashes open and you tumble out of the house.

All right! You made it!

But then you hear the growls around you. You look up.

And you don't like what you see. . . .

Take a look on PAGE 41.

"We aren't crazy!" you cry. "And we aren't letting you go."

"You guys aren't even wearing white coats!" Max chimes in.

The two men growl and thrash, trying to escape. "Let us go, you lunatics!"

Suddenly, something drops from one of the men's pockets.

You reach down and pick it up.

"It's a map!" you announce.

"Great," Max exclaims. "Does it say where we are?"

You peer carefully at the map. You don't recognize any of the places on it. But you notice an X drawn with red marker. Next to the X, some words are written.

"Matter Slammer target," you read.

"What's a Matter Slammer?" Max asks your prisoners.

They just scowl.

"*Slammer*," you murmur to yourself. That word reminds you of something. . . .

Then you see it in your mind. The spinning wheel of fire from your dream. You just *know* it has something to do with the word *slammer*.

But what?

Transport yourself to PAGE 40.

But nothing happens. . . .

Why didn't it work?

"Ha!" an alien laughs. "You didn't think we'd let you destroy another saucer, did you?"

"We turned off the controls," another chimes in. "But you showed us what we need to know. That humans can never be trusted. You were going to destroy another saucer on purpose!"

Uh-oh. Looks like you messed up big this time.

"We've seen humans do some bad things," the first one exclaims. "But this is the *worst*. I guess we'll have to eliminate all humanity, just to make the universe safe."

Your heart starts to pound. *All* humanity?

"Smooth move," Max mutters. "Way to get the human race destroyed."

"But don't worry," an alien adds. "We'll keep you alive so you can watch as we crush your world. And you can remember for the rest of your days that it was *your* fault!"

As the aliens prepare to destroy Earth, you almost wish you could use that memory helmet one more time.

Because you've got a feeling this is one day you'd rather forget. . . .

THE END

"Werewolves!" you shout. You throw the were-wolf-hunting book to one side. "No way!"

"Then why did that silver candlestick burn you?" Max asks.

You frown. You do remember *something* about silver burning werewolves. Actually, that fact seems pretty important to you.

"And why was that woman hunting us with silver arrows?" Max continues. "And why can't we remember who we are?"

"I . . . don't know," you stammer. "Maybe we *are* werewolves. But if we are, let's get out of here before she wakes up."

You dash downstairs, taking the book with you.

You crash out of the front door.

"Boy, am I glad to be out of that house," Max cries.

"Yeah," you agree. "Let's go over to those trees. Then we can read more of this book."

Hidden in the forest, you read about being a werewolf. If the book is right, you go on a crazy rampage every full moon. After the sun comes up, you wake up without any memories.

"That's lousy luck," Max complains. "We get to turn into wolves, but we can't even remember it!"

You start to answer Max. But then your eyes fall on a letter stuck between the pages of the book.

"Uh-oh," you exclaim. "Our luck is worse than you think."

Turn to PAGE 20.

10

Below you are little mountains and houses and forests. Around you are big, pillowy clouds.

Oh, no! You're ten miles up in the air!

And you're starting to . . .

. . . fall.

"Ahhhhh!" Max screams.

"We're in midair!" you shout into the walkie-talkie. "What happened?"

Dr. Sloper's voice crackles from the radio.

"You weren't *supposed* to come back!" she explains. "You were supposed to disappear. That's why I programmed the machine to erase your memories. I sent those goons to capture you. If this project is delayed, I'll have more time to steal the Slammer technology!"

"Oh, no!" Max yells, flailing his arms next to you. "Dr. Sloper is the enemy agent!"

Land on PAGE 37.

You and Max decide to become were-hawks! How can you pass up a chance like this?

You follow the directions in the book carefully. You make a fire, while Max gathers herbs to burn.

Soon, you're all ready to go.

You sit down and read the magic words in the book.

"*Ezzmo, hypho, hawk-varoo,*" the spell begins.

You hope this stuff really works. Otherwise, you're going to feel pretty stupid.

When you're done, Max jumps up, peering into the distance.

"Wow!" he exclaims. "I can see for miles!"

"That makes sense!" you answer. "Birds have great eyesight. I guess we'll find out soon if the spell worked. According to the book, the moon should still be full tonight."

"I can't wait!" Max cries.

"Don't move!" a voice orders from behind you.

Oh, no! Werewolf hunters!

Turn to PAGE 81.

"Problem?" you cry.

"We found *three* helmets," the alien explains. "And we don't know which ones you wore. One of them must contain someone else's memories."

The aliens arrange the helmets in front of you. They're big and black, with menacing spikes all over them.

You gulp. Your memories are trapped in one of those?

Max grabs one of the helmets. "Well, here goes nothing."

He plants it on his head. The helmet starts to hum and shake. Max falls to the ground.

"What happened?" you shout.

An alien peers closely at Max. "Don't worry."

Suddenly, Max's eyes pop open.

"Cool!" he exclaims. "I picked the right one! They're telling the truth. You and I are best friends. We were playing together and the aliens captured us. And wow! What a crash!"

"Your turn," the alien announces.

You glance nervously back and forth between the two helmets. One has your memories. Your whole identity. But which one?

To pick the helmet on the right, turn to PAGE 26.
To pick the one on the left, turn to PAGE 125.

The snake strikes!

Your free hand darts to grab the snake just behind the head.

Got it!

Without a second thought, you toss the snake onto the fence. The barbed wire blazes with sparks!

"Whoa!" Max cries. "Nice going!"

Your nose wrinkles. Yuck! The smell of snake, well-done.

"I told you our reflexes wouldn't let us down," you shout.

Brimming with confidence, you leap from the branch. You clear the fence by a foot.

Yes! You made it!

"Come on!" you order Max.

Max scrambles up the tree. He makes it over the fence with no problem.

"Yeah!" he shouts as he lands gracefully next to you. "It's like we can do anything!"

"Don't move!" a voice from behind you orders.

Hands up on PAGE 30.

THWACK!

The arrow buries itself in the wall a few inches from your head.

Yikes! That was close! You stare at the arrow, frozen for a moment. Its long silver shaft glimmers in the dim light.

"Come on!" Max screams, dragging you down the hall.

You run after him. You hear the dogs charging up the stairs.

You run to the end of the hall, swinging around a turn. In front of you is another staircase leading down toward the back of the house. But Max points upward. There's an attic trapdoor in the ceiling above you.

Going down the stairs will be quicker than climbing up to the attic. But maybe the dogs will lose your scent if you go through the trapdoor.

Which way should you go?

To head up to the attic, climb to PAGE 77.

To head down the back stairs, descend to PAGE 6.

You can't believe your eyes!

The saucer barrels out of the clouds, lit by a row of blinking red lights around its middle. As you gaze up at it, you remember another part of your nightmare . . . the burning wheel of fire.

The saucer looks just like it!

It looks as if your nightmare was *real*!

"What does this all mean?" you shout. "Why are they calling us prisoners? Why do they want to capture us?"

"We can worry about that later!" Max orders. "Right now, we've got a flying saucer to worry about."

You nod your head and peer down at the zapper. Should you try to shoot down the saucer?

Or should you hide before they see you?

To shoot at the saucer, aim for PAGE 93.
To hide, run for PAGE 66.

16

You decide to spy on the hunters *before* you turn into wolves tonight. You head back toward the house.

When the house comes into view, Max's jaw drops.

You gulp. There are a *lot* of hunters arriving. Jeeps and trucks surround the abandoned house. The hunters are setting up tents and standing around comparing werewolf-killing weapons.

"We must be a big deal!" Max exclaims.

You creep up behind one of the Jeeps.

"Look in here!" Max whispers, pointing into the Jeep.

It's a duffel bag full of hunting outfits. *Perfect!*

You and Max climb into the camouflage jackets and pants. The clothes are a little big, but now you'll totally fit in with the hunters.

But then a stern voice booms out behind you.

"Hey, you two," it bellows. "What are you doing over there?"

Gulp. You're busted!

Bust out to PAGE 22.

Dr. Sloper is right in the middle of the Slammer platform.

You dash to the control panel. You push the biggest button you see.

Was it the right one? you wonder.

Dr. Sloper peers down at the spinning lights below her and screams. But the high, screeching noise of the machine drowns her out.

She disappears!

"Whoa!" Max declares. "You sent her ten miles high. Without a parachute!"

"Well, I had to," you explain. "After all, she was *highly* dangerous!"

THE END

18

"Ahwoo!" you howl as you wake up.

Whoa! you think, shaking your furry head. That was some nightmare.

Images from the dream dance in your mind. You actually dreamed you were a human — who turned into a wolf! A werewolf. Creepy.

You remember a bunch of hunters. And a terrible net that you couldn't escape.

What an awful dream!

At least it's over. You're so glad you're just a plain old wolf. And you're happy to be back in your nice warm cave with all the other wolves.

Well, it's time to get back to sleep.

And no more nightmares!

THE END

"Okay," you agree. "Let's see if this map leads anywhere."

"See you guys later," Max calls to the two prisoners.

You head outside. Max points at the sun.

"That's sunrise," he begins. "So it must be east."

He turns the map the right way, peering at the countryside that stretches for miles around you.

"How did you know that?" you ask.

"Remember how we just sort of *knew* how to fight those guys?" he explains. "Well, I bet we know how to read maps and other cool stuff like that too."

You lean over the map and stare carefully at it. The elevation lines and coordinate numbers all make sense to you.

"Cool!" you shout. "You're right!"

Wow! you think. You've got all sorts of neat knowledge in your head. *But where did it come from?*

Then you notice another marking on the map. It reads, SLAMMER PROJECT HEADQUARTERS. Again, you see the spinning wheel of fire in your mind.

You shake the vision out of your head. You plant your finger on the map. "*That's* where we need to go!"

Follow your nose to PAGE 103.

Your heart sinks as you read the letter again. It announces a meeting of all the best werewolf hunters in the world. They're all getting together to hunt the most dangerous werewolves ever — you and Max!

"That crazy hunter just got here early," you explain. "But soon there'll be dozens of them!"

"We're doomed!" Max exclaims.

Then your eyes fall on the book again. "But look at this. The book says we can cure ourselves!"

You keep reading. The book contains lots of spells. Like how to make creepy werewolf-hunting dolls. No thanks!

It also explains how to make yourself into a normal human. Or turn into some other kind of werebeast.

"Cool!" Max exclaims. "Like a were-rhinoceros!"

"Or a were-snake!" you chime in.

"I know!" Max shouts. "We could be werehawks. They'll never catch us if we can fly!"

"Great idea!" you proclaim. "But we'd still lose our memory. Maybe we should become regular people."

What should you do? Cure yourselves completely? Or become were-hawks and fly to safety?

To cure yourselves, turn to PAGE 121.
To become were-hawks, fly to PAGE 11.

You throw yourselves to the floor and roll under the bed.

Just in time!

The door crashes open seconds later. Someone, or some*thing*, steps into the room. The heavy footsteps are mixed with the sound of tiny motors whirring.

You peer out from beneath the bed. The feet seem to be made of shiny black metal. They stomp around the room.

Not over here! you plead silently. Whatever it is, you don't want to meet it face-to-face.

But the feet come closer . . .

And closer . . .

The feet stop, only inches from the bed.

Suddenly, the bed flies up into the air. It crashes to the floor on the other side of the room.

You've been found!

You cover your eyes in panic. But a huge voice booms in your ears.

"Rescue Robot reporting for duty!"

Turn to PAGE 50.

You turn around. In front of you is a huge, burly man. He's armed with a big crossbow made completely of silver.

"Uh . . ." you stall. "We're werewolf hunters!"

"You're a little young to hunt werewolves," he says sarcastically.

"Oh, no!" Max exclaims. "We're experts on wolf-calling."

"Wolf-calling?" The man snorts in disbelief.

"Yeah," Max asserts. "Watch *this*."

He puts his fingers in his mouth and lets out a shrill whistle. Then he screws up his face in concentration.

"Wow!" the hunter cries, peering at the edge of the forest.

You choke down your surprise. Trotting out of the forest are five wolves. Then you realize — Max must have called them with his mind!

The hunter loads his crossbow hastily.

He raises it to fire!

You can't let him hit your new friends. You bump into him as he shoots, muttering, "Oops!" The wolves jump back into the trees.

"Missed," he complains. "But you two are going to be mighty helpful. Welcome to the hunt!"

All right!

Join the hunt on PAGE 49.

With a sickening ripping sound, the drainpipe pulls loose.

"Ahhhhh!" you both scream as you plunge toward the ground.

OOOF!

You find yourself sprawled on the ground. You stand up gingerly. Nothing *seems* broken. Max stands shakily next to you.

Phew! You made it.

You peer back up at the bedroom window. You can't see anything up there.

Your eyes search the field behind the house. Weird wreckage is scattered all over the place.

Then you hear a funny noise. It sounds like a tiny voice talking to you from the grass. You bend down and peer closely at the ground.

There's something down there. . . .

You lift up an object that looks like a little necklace. You hold it up to your ear.

"*Rreechna yaloo varinda!*" it screeches.

Yikes! You almost drop the necklace.

"What language is *that*?" Max asks.

Rreechna yaloo *to PAGE 80.*

You've had enough of this creepy doll dance! *Save us!* you think at the wolf.

The wolf disappears from the window. You tear your eyes back to the dolls reeling around you. Their silver teeth snap as they dance.

You hope that wolf knows what he's doing. . . .

Suddenly, furry shapes fly into the room from every direction. Wolves grab the screaming dolls in their teeth, ripping the stuffing out of them. The hunter flees from the room in a panic.

All right! It's a whole pack of wolves!

You and Max are saved!

The wolves make short work of the dolls. They lead you and Max out of the house and into the forest nearby.

"Whoa!" Max exclaims. "We've got our own wolf pack. Being a werewolf is cool!"

"Yeah," you agree. "As long as there aren't too many more of those werewolf hunters around."

There are lots of werewolf hunters nearby, the wolf leader informs you. *We can smell them coming!*

Great.

Hunt down PAGE 130.

"Ahhhhhh!" you scream.

And then you wake up.

Whoa! you think, shaking your head. That was some nightmare.

Images from the dream dance in your mind. Something about little people only two feet tall. You also remember a huge spinning wheel of fire. And a horrible screeching sound.

What a weird dream! At least you're in your nice warm bed.

That's funny. You're wearing your clothes.

You stretch your arms and yawn.

Hey! What's that written on your hand?

LOOK IN POCKET, it says.

In your pocket are a stubby pencil and some wadded-up toilet paper. There's writing on the paper! You start to read.

And it's the craziest story you've ever heard. About a kid who gets kidnapped by aliens. They try to erase his memory. So he writes the story down — and sticks the paper in his pocket.

It's completely unbelievable. Only a nut would write something like this!

There's only one problem. . . .

It's in *your* handwriting.

THE END

You hand the zapper to Max and pick up the helmet on the right.

"Good luck," Max cries as you put the helmet on.

A humming noise fills your head. The helmet starts to shake. It's rattling your brain!

Then suddenly, memories flood into your head.

That's it! Of course! Now you can remember *exactly* who you are.

You pull the helmet from your head. You grab the zapper back from Max and point it at the aliens.

"Okay! Take us home," you order the aliens.

The aliens obey. After all, you've still got the zapper.

Riding in their saucer, it only takes a few minutes. You land behind a nice country house.

"Home, sweet home," Max shouts.

The aliens leave. You and Max watch the saucer disappear into the sky.

"That was TOTALLY cool!" Max shouts. "Wait until we tell everyone what happened."

"You're not telling anyone anything!" you growl, pointing the zapper at Max.

Turn to PAGE 136.

"Okay. Let's take a peek," you decide.

"I agree," Max answers.

You creep to the top of the stairs.

"There!" Max whispers, pointing downward.

At the bottom of the rickety stairs is the front door of the house. You flinch as the banging starts again. The door shakes with every knock.

Max gulps. "Whoever is down there must be pretty strong!"

"Don't let them see you!" you warn.

Max crouches down behind the stair rails. You drop to the floor, peeking over the topmost step.

A muffled whining comes from below.

"Is that a dog?" Max whispers.

You shrug your shoulders.

Then a high voice counts, "One, two, *three!*"

With a crash, the door bursts open.

Turn to PAGE 95.

The soldiers lower their weapons. The woman rushes up and shakes your hand.

"Congratulations!" she exclaims. "I'm so glad it worked! How far did you go?"

"Uh —" you stammer. What's she talking about?

"We don't remember anything!" Max blurts out.

"About slamming?" she asks.

"About *anything*!" you cry. "We just woke up. It feels like we had a bad dream or something. We don't know what really happened. We don't even know who we are!"

"Oh, dear," she mutters. "You better get on the truck. It looks like there's been some side effects. The Slammer must have damaged your brain!"

Brain damage again. Great.

Turn to PAGE 92.

You decide to lure the humans out a few at a time.

Hidden at the edge of the hunters' busy camp, you make a whimpering sound.

"Is that a dog out there?" one of the hunters asks.

"Let's go see," another suggests.

The hunters creep out into the dark night. They have silver knives drawn. But you're ready for them!

You and Max spring out of the darkness. You crash straight into the hunters.

"Oooof!" they grunt. They fall to the ground, unconscious.

You remind yourself not to yelp out a victory howl. There are plenty more hunters to go tonight.

You and Max nip the dazed hunters. Soon, they start to grow fur of their own. They wake up and join the hunt!

It takes all night. A few at a time, the hunters are transformed into werewolves. Dozens of them.

Then the party really starts! You howl at the moon all night. You play-fight like wolf cubs.

This was a great idea. You're one big werewolf family!

When dawn comes, you and your new werewolf brothers and sisters crawl into the abandoned house. Time to sleep . . .

Wake up on PAGE 99.

You put your hands in the air and turn around. A soldier holds a club at the ready.

Uh-oh. He looks a lot tougher than the snake!

"Who are you?" the soldier demands.

"Uh . . ." you stall. "I guess . . . I don't know."

"What?" he snaps.

"You see, we woke up in some old house," Max explains. "But we couldn't remember anything except we could do cool things. And these guys came to get us and they had a map —"

"Quiet!" the soldier orders. "This is a top-secret base. You two are in *big* trouble."

Keeping a stern eye on you both, the soldier pulls a two-way radio out of his pocket.

"This is Unit Five," he barks into the radio.

Oh, no! He's calling for help. What should you do?

You could try to disarm him. After all, you can move faster than a snake! Or you can just let him take you to whoever's in charge here. Maybe *they* know what's going on.

What will it be?

To try to disarm the guard, turn to PAGE 76.
To let yourself be taken in, turn to PAGE 106.

When you wake up, you're in a huge circular room. There are windows all around you. You peer through them and gasp.

Clouds are rushing by! You must be going about a thousand miles an hour!

You stand up shakily. Max is right next to you.

"Do those guys look familiar or what?" he asks.

You follow his gaze. Three little figures are staring back at you. They're only two feet tall! Their long arms brush the floor of the saucer.

"Just like in that nightmare!" you cry.

"They're definitely aliens," Max declares. "Oh, man!"

"*Kwashoo motar*," one of the aliens sputters. Then it reaches to its throat and adjusts a necklace there.

"Caught you again!" the necklace translates.

Just great. It sounds as if you and Max have been here before!

Turn to PAGE 78.

"Our help?" you stammer.

"You were working on a top-secret project," the man explains. "A machine that could send people miles away in the blink of an eye. A Matter Slammer!"

"You're nuts," you respond. But the word *slammer* rings a bell. You remember the spinning wheel of fire from your nightmare. Could the man be telling the truth?

"You were the first test subjects," he continues. "But we sabotaged the experiment. You were sent to an empty house. And we programmed the Slammer to erase your memories."

This stinks! You're a secret agent, and you can't even remember it.

"Why?" Max demands.

"We wanted you to disappear," he explains. "So that your government would think the device didn't work. We wanted you to help us to create our own Slammer."

"Then you shouldn't have erased our memories!" you object.

"Oh, we don't need your minds," he scoffs. "Just your bodies. You see, *our* Slammer has this problem. . . ."

He opens the door behind him. A strange, horrible creature slinks into the room. It's half dog and half snake!

Hisssswoof! it yelps.

Turn to PAGE 118.

The attic is full of stuff. Dusty old toys and leather-bound books and ancient furniture surround you. Weird shapes lurk under the sheets that cover them.

"It looks like no one's been here for a hundred years!" Max whispers.

"Maybe we can find something we can use to fight that crazy woman," you suggest.

"Good idea!" Max agrees.

You both search the attic. You move slowly in the darkness, careful not to make too much noise.

A pair of big, thick silver candlesticks catches your eye. You could totally brain someone with them.

"Check these out!" you exclaim. You reach for one of the candlesticks.

But as your hand closes around the candlestick, a sudden fiery pain leaps through your body. It's like touching a hot iron!

"Ahhhhh!" you scream, dropping the candlestick.

Turn to PAGE 57.

You decide to go downstairs and find out who's there. Maybe they know who you are.

"Come on," you order Max.

The knocking continues as you clomp down the stairs.

"We're coming!" you yell. Whoever it is, they sure are impatient.

Suddenly, the door flies open with a *CRASH!* Splinters of wood fly through the air.

Two huge men in black suits tumble through the door. They're wearing black sunglasses, and their muscular bodies are almost bursting out of their suits.

Who are these guys? you wonder.

The men take one look at you and Max and grab you both in crushing grips. They lift you from the floor.

"Got you!" one bellows.

Uh-oh.

Turn to PAGE 96.

Aiming carefully, you press the red button.

And nothing happens.

The zapper says something in the weird language. Is it out of ammo?

"Self-destruct sequence engaged," the necklace translates. "Prepare for major explosion."

Self-destruct sequence? *Major explosion!*

Uh-oh.

You push the red button again. It won't pop back up! You pound it with your finger.

There! The necklace is translating something again!

You put your ear up to it.

"Five, four, three . . ." it counts down.

You turn to run, but you guess you won't get very far in three seconds.

And you don't. . . .

THE END

You feebly raise your hands. But the rain of old furniture hits you like a ton of bricks.

"Ark," you croak from beneath the junk.

"Oh, dear," the hunter sighs. "There's nothing more dangerous that a wounded werewolf!"

Werewolf? Is *that* what you are?

You try to move, but you can hardly even breathe.

The hunter notches another silver-tipped arrow onto her bow and takes careful aim at your chest.

And she said she was going to cure you.

Guess you *fell* for that one pretty bad!

THE END

You gulp, watching the ground rushing up to meet you.

"But this time, I've gotten rid of you for sure!" Dr. Sloper taunts through the walkie-talkie.

"Any chance you could slam us a parachute?" you plead.

Dr. Sloper just laughs, and the walkie-talkie goes silent.

"This is all your fault!" Max screams. "I wanted to catch the spy first!"

But you think that you and Max should share the blame.

After all, you both *fell* for it. . . .

Happy landings!

THE END

After the crash, you and Max must have wandered into the empty house, dazed by the memory-stealing helmets.

"So *that's* what happened!" Max exclaims.

"Tell us what you did to crash the saucer!" the alien orders. "We must prevent another accident."

"Then we can erase your memories of meeting us again," another alien chimes in.

"Hey, that wasn't part of the deal!" you shout.

"We promised to let you go," the alien corrects you. "We never said anything about you keeping your memories!"

"This stinks!" Max complains.

Max is right. You've been captured by aliens — *twice!* — and now they want you to forget it again.

A plan comes into your mind. You know which button to push to make the saucer crash. You could just press the same button. This time you could take the helmet off before you crashed — and keep your memory!

But you made a deal. And maybe it's not such a good idea to make the saucer crash. This time, you might not survive. Is there a way you can keep your memories without crashing the saucer?

What should you do?

To make the saucer crash, turn to PAGE 90.

To think of another way to keep your memories, try PAGE 110.

You spring the trap! You hurl the door open and send the tower of stuff tumbling down.

CRASH!

The hunter disappears, buried under the avalanche of junk.

"All right!" Max cries. "You got her!"

You jump down in triumph.

The hunter's tools are scattered all over the hall. The deadly arrows, the weird dolls, and other stuff you don't even recognize.

Max sees something interesting and picks it up.

"Whoa! Look at this book!" he cries.

You read the words on the cover. *How to Hunt Werewolves.*

Werewolves!

Is that the awful disease the hunter was talking about?

Turn to PAGE 9.

"At least we know one thing," Max proclaims. 'We didn't escape from a mental hospital. I mean, *slammer target*? Whatever's going on is weirder than just being crazy."

Max grabs the map from you.

"Maybe we can figure out where we are from this map," he suggests.

"How?" you ask.

"We search the area to see if anything looks like it's on the map," he explains. "Like a big hill or something. Then we go from there."

"I don't know," you argue. "I think we should stay here and look around. There's bound to be more clues somewhere in this house."

What should you do? Use the map to figure out where you are? Or search the house for more clues?

To try to use the map, find yourself on PAGE 19.
To search the house, look for PAGE 129.

A pack of dogs surrounds you. Their spiked collars glint in the sunlight. But that's not the scariest part.

Riding the dogs are little dolls, about two feet tall. They clutch the spiked collars with weirdly long arms.

Just like in that nightmare! you realize. You remember the little figures from the dream, their long arms dragging on the floor.

"What are you?" you cry.

In a horrible, high voice, one of the dolls squeaks, "We were made to kill werewolves!"

"Werewolves?" you whimper. "But we aren't —"

"Let's get out of here!" Max yells. "Back into the house!"

"No way," you answer. You point at the forest, a short distance away. "Let's run for the trees."

The dolls order their dogs forward.

"Wh-wh-which way?" Max stammers.

What should you do? Run back into the house? Or head for the forest?

To run back into the house, turn to PAGE 71.
To head for the trees, run to PAGE 91.

You decide to play along.

"Okay!" you exclaim. "Just get it over with!"

"It won't take long," the man declares. "The Slammer is almost ready."

He leaves, taking the terrible snake-dog with him.

"We're doomed!" Max wails.

"Maybe not," you mutter. "After all, we're some kind of secret agents, working on a top-secret project, right?

"That's why we have these super-fast reflexes," Max agrees.

"So why don't we have any cool secret gadgets to help us out of jams?" you complain.

"Maybe we do!" Max exclaims. "We just don't remember them!"

"You're right," you agree.

You and Max struggle in your handcuffs, trying to find anything that you're carrying secretly.

After a moment, Max cries, "The heel on my shoe is loose!"

He pulls it off. Inside is some kind of small metal device. It's covered with tiny circuits and lights.

"Jackpot!" you cry.

"Yeah," Max agrees. "But what does it *do*?"

Find out on PAGE 84.

You squint your eyes as you squeeze the blue button. . . .

ZAAAP!

A blue ray leaps from the zapper, slamming straight into the saucer.

"Yes!" Max shouts. "Direct hit!"

But the saucer doesn't explode. A blinding beam shoots from the saucer. It hits your beam — and bounces it back toward you!

Uh-oh, you think.

You hold the weapon steady, squeezing the button as hard as you can. Maybe your ray will break through. . . .

But the saucer's beam pushes yours back, closer and closer to you! It's about to hit you!

Zap your way to PAGE 73.

You whip your hand out from behind your back, with two fingers showing.

Max also has two fingers showing. . . .

"Two plus two is four!" Max cries triumphantly. "That's even, so you're the bait. Excellent!"

"Yeah, great," you sigh. "Next time, we're doing rock-paper-scissors!"

You press your ear to the attic door. Not a sound. You open the door and unfold the ladder, creeping quietly down to the hallway. Above you, Max peeks out through a tiny crack.

"Owww!" you wail. You collapse on the floor. "My leg! I can't run anymore!"

You yell once more as if in awful pain. The hunter appears at the top of the stairs. Her bow is already cocked, with one of the silver arrows aimed right at you.

She peers warily at you. "Where's the other one?"

"Uh, I don't know," you stammer.

Don't look at the attic door! you order yourself.

The hunter takes a few steps forward, her aim never wavering. She's right under the attic door!

"Now!" you shout.

Don't just lie there. Turn to PAGE 97.

"Wow! Those guys were five times bigger than us," Max proclaims. "And we *toasted* them!"

"No kidding," you agree. "But what does this all mean? How were we able to fight like that?"

"Do you think we're karate experts?" you ask.

"So why would these guys be after karate experts?" Max answers. "Do you think we overcharged them for lessons?"

"Maybe not," you admit. "But we better find out soon. In case there are more people out to get us."

Max gulps. "You're right. Let's get out of here before they wake up. I'm not sure I can do all that karate stuff again."

"Why don't we tie them up?" you suggest. "When they come to, we can ask them what's going on."

"Maybe," Max says. "But there might be clues upstairs where we woke up. Something that would explain who we are."

You can tie the men up and wait for them to awake. Or you can look upstairs for clues.

What should you do?

To tie the men up and ask them questions, turn to PAGE 126.

To look upstairs for clues, turn to PAGE 137.

Ahwooo! One of the dogs starts howling. It's a high, horrible sound. And you remember it all too well.

It's the terrible screeching sound from your dream!

You peek down the stairs. The dogs are staring right back at you.

The woman peers up the stairs.

"Don't move!" she shouts.

Oh, no! You're busted!

You and Max spring to your feet.

BONK! Your heads collide with a painful crunch. You stumble a moment, trying not to fall down the stairs. You grab the banister at the last moment.

The woman below is calmly drawing back her bow and arrow.

She's going to shoot you!

You throw yourself backwards as she takes aim . . .

. . . and fires!

Turn to PAGE 14.

"Let's use the machine again," you decide.

You want your memories back!

Max hesitates, then reluctantly joins you on the Slammer platform.

"This better work!" he demands.

Dr. Sloper sends everyone else out of the lab.

"You never know who the enemy agent might be!" she explains.

She gives you a walkie-talkie.

"Just call me after you arrive," she orders.

The lights on the platform start to spin. You close your eyes. The machine starts to whine.

Wow! It's just like the high-pitched screech in your dream.

You just wonder where you'll wind up this time!

The screech gets louder and louder. Your hair is standing on end. Soon, you feel your feet lifting up from the platform, as if some huge magnet were pulling you up!

Suddenly, there's a huge *POP* in your ears.

You open your eyes. The lab has disappeared! Where are you?

Find yourself on PAGE 10.

48

You throw open the window. You're getting out of here!

You climb out, holding on to the window frame for dear life. Your feet scrape against the side of the house. You search for a foothold.

But there's nothing between you and the ground.

Yikes! Maybe you should have looked for a way down *before* you jumped out the window.

Then you see a drainpipe a few feet from you. If you can just reach it, you can climb down!

You stretch one arm out. . . .

Got it! All right!

Dangling from one hand, you swing over to the drainpipe. You start to lower yourself carefully to the ground.

Then you hear a creaking sound. You peer up. Max is right above you.

But the drainpipe is starting to come loose!

"Wait!" you scream. "The pipe can't hold us both!"

Max glances around in horror. He tries to reach the windowsill again. But the pipe wrenches away from the side of the house.

You're going to fall!

Fall toward PAGE 23.

"Good idea," you whisper to Max when the hunter is out of earshot.

"Now the hunters will totally trust us," Max responds.

Soon the hunt gets started. Dozens of hunters head into the woods together, forming a long line. As the world's best wolf callers, you and Max are in the lead.

Of course, you're really *helping* the wolves, using your minds to warn them of the hunters' approach. The wolf pack howls every once in a while to make you look good. But it's always from a safe distance.

"After a few more days of this," you whisper to Max, "the hunters will get pretty frustrated."

"Then maybe they'll go away and leave us alone!" Max agrees.

Already, some of the hunters are grumbling.

You come to a tall hill.

"Up this way!" Max orders. He smiles slyly at you. You both know there aren't any wolves for miles!

But when you reach the top of the hill, you get a nasty surprise.

The full moon is rising!

Rise to the occasion on PAGE 132.

"Wh-what?" you stammer.

You open your eyes. You can hardly believe what you see.

Towering over you is a huge figure. It's shaped like a human, with two arms and legs, but made of black metal. Its body is covered with strange, unreadable markings.

"Rescue Robot reporting," it repeats. "Are you injured?"

"Uh, n-no," Max answers. "What's going on?"

"You are the only survivors of the crash," the robot announces.

"What crash?" you ask.

"I received a distress call one hour ago," it explains. "Saucer Forty-three was falling, out of control."

"Wow!" you cry. "We must have hit our heads in the crash. No wonder we don't remember anything."

"Wait a second," your friend demands. "How did we get a flying saucer?"

"It is not your saucer," the robot explains. "You are our prisoners. Now you have been captured again."

The robot extends a metal arm, and a yellow gas sprays out over you.

"Wait!" you cry. But before you can say another word, your head is spinning.

Then everything goes black. . . .

Turn to PAGE 31.

"Run for it!" you yell.

Taken by surprise, the hunters fall back out of your way. You burst through the circle of hunters, dashing into the thick trees.

You risk one quick glance backwards.

All right! Max is right behind you!

But soon you hear the shouts of your pursuers. Arrows whistle past you. Rifle shots ring out.

You hear a grunt behind you, and a thud.

Oh, no! Max has been hit!

You keep running, but out of the corner of your eye you see a flashing shape coming at you through the trees. It looks like some kind of metal bird.

Yikes! It's the silver boomerang!

THWAP! It smacks right into your chest.

"Ahhh!" you scream, falling to the forest floor.

Your sight starts to fade. The silver is working its terrible magic on you.

You're done for!

Turn to PAGE 128.

You decide to walk along the fence.

"There's got to be a way in," Max declares.

The fence seems to stretch for miles. But you and Max keep walking. Your instincts tell you that the secret to your missing memory is somewhere on this base. You can still see the spinning wheel of fire from your nightmare. If you can get past this fence, you're certain you'll find out who you are.

Pretty soon, you come to a gate. A soldier stands guard in a sentry box. The moment he spots you, he steps out.

"What are you two doing here?" he demands.

"Uh, we need to talk to someone on this base," you explain.

"Who?" the guard barks, lifting a phone in the sentry box.

"Uh," you stall. "I can't remember. . . ."

The guard's eyes widen, but before he can bark at you again, a long car pulls up at the gate.

"Wait here!" he commands, and turns to the car.

You catch a glimpse of the driver as the window opens.

Yikes! It's one of the men in black suits! They must have escaped. . . .

Turn to PAGE 88.

"Wake up!" a voice commands.

Still groggy from the wolfsbane, you struggle to open your eyes. Max is right next to you. The rest of the room comes slowly into focus.

"Yikes!" you croak. You're surrounded by tiny people! Little two-foot-tall figures, just like in your dream!

You shake your head to clear your vision, and peer at the figures. Phew! They're only dolls. They're on every side of you and Max, their long arms linked in a circle around you.

Their silver teeth send shivers up your spine.

The crazy werewolf-hunting woman stands outside the circle.

"Wake up!" she repeats. "It's time to complete the ritual."

"What ritual?" you ask.

"I'm going to cure you of being a werewolf," she answers.

"But we're not werewolves!" Max complains.

"You just don't *know* you're werewolves," the woman corrects him. "At every full moon you go on a terrible rampage. But when you wake up the next morning, you don't remember anything."

Uh-oh! you think. Could this be true?

Turn to PAGE 107.

After Max explains his plan to you, you realize he's TOTALLY right! Everyone *has* to believe you.

With the deadly zapper, you force the aliens to take you home. Then you release your hostage. The aliens shoot off into the sky.

You and Max call the newspapers and TV stations. At first the reporters won't listen. But then you stick the memory helmets on their heads ...

And they "remember" everything that happened to *you*!

You and Max are the first people to be kidnapped by aliens who can actually prove it. Soon, you're both rich and famous.

And every night you stare up at the stars and say, "Thanks for the memories."

THE END

"Prisoners!" Max shouts in disbelief. "Why were we prisoners?"

"And *who's* after us?" you add.

You both stare at the zapper.

"You know," Max says in a small voice. "That thing doesn't look like anything on Earth."

You gulp. Aliens? That *can't* be it!

But you can't tear your eyes from the zapper. And what about the strange wreckage? And that floating robot head . . . ?

Suddenly, you hear a high, screeching noise coming from the sky.

"That sound!" Max cries. "I remember it!"

He's right! It sounds like the noise in your nightmare, right before you woke up!

You peer upward, and you almost choke with fear.

A flying saucer is coming toward you. . . .

Fly to PAGE 15.

"Noooowoof!" you yowl.

You're in an open field with Max.

All right! The Matter Slammer must have worked.

You escaped!

But Max is staring at you in total horror.

"What's the matt-hiss?" you ask.

"Ahhhh!" he screams, running away from you.

And it doesn't take you long to figure out why. The claws and scales are a dead giveaway. Not to mention the horrible hissing that comes out of your mouth.

Which makes this a *very* mixed-up . . .

END.

Max clamps a hand over your mouth, cutting off your scream.

"Be quiet!" he whispers.

You peer at your hand through tears of pain. Then you show the palm to Max.

His mouth drops open. "Whoa! It's totally burned!"

You stare at the candlestick. It glimmers with silver light in the darkness. Suddenly, you remember the gleaming arrow that the crazy hunter shot at you.

"That candlestick is silver!" you exclaim.

"So what?" Max asks.

"The arrow that crazy woman shot at me was also silver," you explain.

"But why would silver burn you?" he asks.

"I don't *know*," you whine. You feel yourself starting to panic. "But I don't want to get trapped up here. Let's sneak down."

"I've got a better idea," Max disagrees. "Let's set a trap for her. We can lure her underneath the attic door, then drop a whole bunch of this old junk down onto her head."

Should you try to sneak out of the house? Or lay a trap for the hunter?

To sneak down, creep to PAGE 83.
To set a crushing trap, turn to PAGE 75.

You crash into the fence.

ZZZZAAAP!

You're stuck to the fence, slowly frying! You gasp for breath.

A swarm of images flows into your mind. Somehow, the shock is restoring your memory!

You and Max are secret agents! You're in a special agent program for kids. You volunteered for an experiment, a test of something called a Matter Slammer. The machine worked. It slammed you right through space. You traveled miles in the blink of an eye.

Too bad it accidentally erased your memories! And too bad the enemy agents found you first. Because you're cooked!

THE END

The little doll's teeth plunge into your flesh. It feels like the teeth are red-hot. Smoke is pouring from your wound!

"Ahhhh!" You fall to the ground screaming and trying to rip the doll from your leg. Max grabs it and yanks it backwards, throwing it into the air.

You try to stand, but your leg hurts too much. It looks like you were burned with a blowtorch!

The dogs and their terrible little riders surround you and Max, growling and screeching.

You're done for!

Then another howling sound comes from across the field.

"What now?" Max whimpers.

Suddenly, a pack of wolves springs from the trees. They're coming straight at you! The dogs growl nervously, backing away. The wolves plunge into the dog pack. They grab the dolls in their teeth and rip them to pieces.

Soon the dogs are in full retreat. The few remaining dolls cling to their dogs for dear life.

"All right!" you cry.

But then the wolves turn and stare at you and Max.

"Uh, nice wolves?" Max stammers.

If you're not too dog-tired, turn to PAGE 109.

"Push the EMER button!" you command. "I've got a good feeling about that one."

Max pushes it, and steps back from the device.

BEEP, BEEP, it beeps.

"It's getting ready to do something cool," you promise.

It keeps on beeping for a while.

"Pretty cool," Max snorts. "I'm going to try the other one."

Before he can reach for the device, the door bursts open! The bad guys grab you and Max and rip the beeping device from his hand.

"Take them to the Slammer," someone orders. You and Max are dragged from the room.

"Great guess," Max complains. "Why did I listen to you?"

When you reach the huge Slammer device, you whistle. It almost fills up an entire room. It's a huge circle of lights.

Whoa! It looks like the wheel of fire in your dream!

They throw you and Max onto the Slammer.

"Great!" he rails. "We're going to get turned into a horrible monster."

They turn the huge machine on. . . .

Turn to PAGE 133.

"Look at me!" you scream. Fur is sprouting all over your body. Max is also growing black and white hair everywhere.

You find yourself changing, shrinking.

You glare at the sorceress. "Your cure didn't work!"

"Oh, but it did," the magic woman laughs. "It worked perfectly. You're not a werewolf anymore."

"Are you crazy?" you try to scream, but your new sharp teeth get in the way. A huge tail is sprouting from you.

But then you peer over at Max, and understand. He's very small, with a little black snout and a long black-and-white tail.

He's a skunk!

You've both been turned into were-skunks!

One thing's for sure. . . .

This cure stinks!

THE END

Suddenly, you find yourself in an empty field.

Wow! The Slammer must have worked! You must be miles away from the enemy agent's hide-out.

"Excellent!" you shout triumphantly. The paralysis gas must be wearing off.

"Not so loud!" Max complains.

You turn your head. He's standing right next to you.

Or is he . . . ?

His head is attached to your shoulder! You've only got one body between you!

"Stop shouting!" he yells.

"You're the one who's shouting!" you yell back at him.

"Yeah, well you started it," Max insists.

You can already tell you and Max are going to spend a lot of time arguing.

Who says two heads are better than one?

THE END

"Let's just hide," you decide. "There's no sense taking chances."

"Okay," Max agrees.

You take the lead, edging down the hallway toward the room you're going to hide in. The floor of the old house creaks with every step.

Keep quiet! you order yourself.

The banging downstairs stops.

Oh, no! Did they hear the creaking floor?

You both freeze for a moment, pressed against the wall. You listen as hard as you can, but you don't hear a thing.

"Keep going!" Max whispers after a moment.

You creep slowly forward again, and finally reach the room. You softly push the door open.

Peek into PAGE 86.

"Ahhh!" you yell. You run through the gas, trying to breathe. But the terrible smell is making you faint.

You fall to the ground.

Max coughs as if he's choking to death. He falls heavily on top of you.

You can't breathe!

The woman steps from one of the doorways. She's holding a spray can. She sprays another cloud of smoke at you.

"I knew you'd come out sooner or later," she taunts.

You clutch your throat, trying to breathe.

She waves her hand. "Oh, don't worry about the wolfsbane. It won't kill you."

"Wolfsbane?" you manage to croak. What in the world is *wolfsbane*?

"It'll just make you sleep for a while," she explains. "I always carry lots of it . . . when I'm hunting werewolves."

Werewolves?

Your vision blurs, and everything goes black.

Wake up on PAGE 53.

Dr. Sloper must be the enemy agent! you realize.

"B-b-but," Max stammers. "Why would you mess up your own experiment?"

"I was going to sell the Slammer technology," she explains. "Another government offered me millions!"

"So you made the machine erase our memories?" you ask.

"And sent those goons to capture you," she adds. "If you never came back from the experiment, no one would dare use the machine again!"

"Then you would be the only person who knew that it worked!" Max adds.

"But you found your way back anyhow!" she complains. She reaches over and presses a button. The machine starts to hum. "But you won't be coming back this time!"

"What do you mean?" Max asks.

"I'm going to slam you ten miles up into thin air!" she announces.

Gulp! You suddenly remember something about yourself. . . .

You're afraid of heights!

Land on PAGE 120.

You decide to hide. Maybe the saucer hasn't seen you yet.

"This way!" you order Max.

You dash for the cover of a few nearby trees. Max follows. You both throw yourselves to the ground.

The saucer moves slowly across the field. Your teeth clench as it passes right over you. . . .

And keeps going!

All right! The saucer didn't see you!

But then it banks and turns, getting lower and lower.

"It's landing!" Max whispers.

The saucer settles in the field. A hatch opens and five tiny figures get out. They're only about two feet tall. Their long arms almost reach the ground.

"Whoa!" you mutter. "Just like in my nightmare."

"Mine too," Max agrees.

The figures spread out across the field.

Uh-oh. One's coming your way!

He peers intently down at some sort of instrument in his hands. Suddenly, he points at you and shouts, "Over there!"

No! They've found you!

Turn to PAGE 129.

What a bad dream!

You remember waking up in an abandoned house with no memories. Then these crazy guys in black suits were trying to capture you. And when they finally got you . . .

They put handcuffs on you. Just like the ones you're wearing right now!

And put you in a dark room. With Max, who is lying next to you.

Oh, no! It was *not* a dream!

Too bad. You were sort of hoping it was.

"Wake up!" a voice commands.

Your eyes finally adjust to the dark. A man in a black suit is standing in front of you.

"We need your help," he announces.

Help yourself to PAGE 32.

"Will they eat us?" Max cries.

"I don't kn-kn-know," you stammer, fumbling for the book. "Shouldn't they like us because we're werewolves?"

The wolves surround you. When they smile you can see their long, cruel teeth.

The biggest wolf sits before you. It stares into your eyes. You feel weird. It's almost as if . . . you can hear its thoughts!

We are here to serve you, Masters, it thinks.

"Whoa!" Max shouts. "Did you hear that!"

"Yeah," you respond. "Pretty cool. Now we don't have to worry about any werewolf hunters interrupting us."

You stare at the wolf pack leader. "Make sure no one sneaks up on us!" you order. The leader nods.

You turn back to the smoking fire. You read the magic words from the book. When you're done, your hand itches like crazy. The palm where you were burned by the silver candlestick is starting to heal!

"I think it's working," Max proclaims.

You nod your head. But then you hear a horrible growl behind you. You turn around.

It's the wolf pack leader! And it doesn't look happy!

Turn to PAGE 124.

"Ahhhhhh!" you scream.

You both turn and run. You tear blindly through the charred wreckage. Your heart pounds in your chest. Is the floating head catching up with you? You want to turn. But you're too scared to look!

Whoops! Your foot catches on a piece of the wreckage. You tumble to the ground. Somehow, you've got to stand back up. You have to keep running!

Ouch! Your ankle is twisted. You fall down again.

"I can't run!" you cry. Max skids to a halt.

You glance back. The head is coming straight at you!

Oh, no!

Then you see what you tripped over. It looks like a TV antenna from someone's roof. Except it has a remote to aim it with. Could it be some kind of . . . zapper-ray weapon?

You grab the device and point it at the head.

"Stop!" you cry. "Or I'll shoot!"

The head keeps coming. Open fire!

Then you realize that the zapper doesn't have a trigger.

Instead, it has two buttons. One red and one blue.

Which should you push?

To push the blue button, go to PAGE 123.
To push the red button, shoot for PAGE 35.

"Come on!" you yell to Max, and dash through the gate.

You head down the road as fast as you can. In the distance, you can see a low concrete building. Somehow, it seems familiar.

"I've been there before!" Max cries.

"Me too," you agree breathlessly. You're really excited now. You just know you're about to find out what's going on.

But then you hear a car engine behind you. You glance back.

Uh-oh! It's the man in the black suit. He's plowing down the road after you!

"Run faster!" you scream. But the car thunders closer and closer . . .

WHOOSH! It missed you by inches!

It roars past you and squeals to a stop, barring your path.

The man leaps from the car.

"Hey, we beat you up last time!" Max threatens. "Don't make us do it again!"

The man just smiles and raps on the top of the car.

Five more huge men in black suits get out.

Yikes! You've got a feeling that *this* time, getting rid of them won't be so easy. . . .

Turn to PAGE 82.

You decide to run back into the house. After all, those little dolls look deadly!

You stumble back into the kitchen. One of the dogs leaps after you. But Max slams the door in its face.

Phew!

You peer up the stairs, but no one's there.

"Where did she go?" you wonder out loud.

"I don't know," Max answers. "Let's head for the front door!"

You creep down another hall, hoping it leads out of this house. But *not* to any dog-riding dolls!

Suddenly, you hear a *SWOOSH* sound.

"Ouch!" Max yelps, swatting his neck. You peer closely at his neck. You reach over and pull out a little dart.

"What is it?" he demands.

"I don't know," you answer.

SWOOSH!

Ow! Something's stuck in your arm! Another dart!

And you're starting to feel funny. . . .

Dart your way to PAGE 102.

"We're not dangerous lunatics," Max scoffs.

"Not dangerous?" the man protests. "You're dangerous enough to beat up men twice your size!"

He's right! You and Max reacted like trained killers.

"But why erase our memories?" Max argues.

"We were going to teach you to be normal," the man explains. "But first, we had to get rid of your warped personalities."

"Let us go!" the other man chimes in. "You escaped before the treatment was complete. If you don't come back with us, you could suffer permanent brain damage!"

Your mind is spinning. You have no memories. How can you know what's real? If you *are* a dangerous lunatic, you should let them cure you. But what if they're lying?

"Should we let them go?" Max asks.

What'll it be? Let them go? Or try to figure out what's going on without their help?

To let the men go, untie them on PAGE 112.

To figure out who you are without their help, turn to PAGE 7.

The saucer's beam smashes into your weapon. *BZZZT!*

You fly through the air, landing with a loud *WHUMPH!*

Ouch! That felt as if you were kicked by a mule!

But you're not going to give up yet. You reach for the zapper. Uh-oh! It's broken into two pieces.

You're doomed!

"Come on!" Max yells, dragging you to your feet.

You start to run, pounding your way across the field. But the saucer looms over you. A huge door on its underside opens up. It starts to descend.

It's going to swallow you both!

A yellow light surrounds you. You start to feel drowsy.

"Keep running," Max says thickly. But your strength is sucked from your body. You both fall.

As your sight fades, you hear voices from the necklace again.

"We have recaptured the prisoners," one voice announces.

"Make sure they *don't escape again*," another answers.

Turn to PAGE 31.

"Forget it!" you scream, hurling yourself at the man.

You crash into his stomach.

"Ooof!" He crumples to the floor.

"Come on!" you yell, running past the man and through the only door in the room. Max follows hard on your heels.

You stumble through the hallways of the secret hideout. With these handcuffs on, you can hardly keep your balance!

"They escaped!" voices shout from all directions. You hear the *GRRRRISSS* of the dog-snake following you.

"We've got to hide!" Max cries.

"In here!" you yell, stumbling into an open doorway.

You bolt inside. Max slams the door behind you. You both peer around the room and realize where you are.

"Ooops!" Max exclaims.

In front of you is a spinning wheel of fire. . . .

Spin your way to PAGE 114.

You and Max decide to set a trap. After all, if that crazy woman is going to hunt you, you might as well hunt *her*!

As quietly as you can, you pile up a bunch of old furniture beside the trapdoor. Max carefully tests the unsteady heap.

"One push and this will tumble down like an avalanche!" he announces.

You scratch your head. "But how do we lure her under the trapdoor?"

"Well," Max explains, "one of us could pretend to be injured. Then she'd come looking."

"And the other one shoves the pile down onto her!" you finish.

"The only question is, who's going to be the bait?" Max asks.

You gulp. Not you, you hope. "How about Odds or Evens?"

"What's that?" Max asks.

"Here's how it works," you explain. "At the same time, we both put out either two or three fingers. If the total number of fingers is even, I'm the bait. If it's odd, you are."

"Okay, so you're even, I'm odd," Max agrees, putting one hand behind his back. "One, two, three . . . go!"

To put out two fingers, turn to PAGE 44.
To put out three fingers, turn to PAGE 85.

You decide to disarm the soldier. He's no match for your lightning reflexes.

"Come in, Unit Five," his radio crackles. The soldier's eyes glance down at it for a split second.

Now! you think. You leap into action!

You dart forward and rip the club from the soldier's hand. It flies high through the air, landing on the other side of the fence. You grab the soldier's arm in an unbreakable judo hold.

"Hah! Works every time!" you announce to Max.

But the soldier spins out of your grip!

Uh-oh! You got a little too cocky. . . .

He grabs your shoulders and tips backwards, pulling you with him. You fall forward as he rolls onto his back.

With one foot planted in your chest, he throws you over his head!

"Aaaahhhh!" you scream as you hurtle through the air.

Yikes! You're headed right for the electric fence!

You're in for a jolt on **PAGE 58.**

You jump up and grab the attic door. Your weight pulls it open. A ladder unfolds downward.

You and Max scramble up the ladder. At the top, you reach down and pull the ladder up. The door closes behind you.

The howling dogs pause for a moment right underneath you. You can hear them snuffling and whining in confusion.

All right! They've lost your scent.

You hold your breath, hoping the woman doesn't spot the attic door.

Then the sound of the dogs fades away.

"Phew!" Max whispers. "We made it!"

"But why are they hunting us?" you ask.

"I don't know." Max sighs wearily. "But did you hear the horrible sound those dogs made?"

"It's like the screeching sound in my nightmare," you declare.

"Mine too!" Max exclaims. "But why? Was our dream real?"

"Search me," you say. "None of this makes any sense."

You peer around the gloomy attic.

"Wow!" you murmur.

Turn to PAGE 33.

"What's going on here?" Max demands.

"You destroyed one of our saucers!" the alien proclaims.

"We did?" Max sputters. "But we don't remember anything!"

"Of course you don't!" the alien snaps. "We always erase our captives' memories. Otherwise they'd tell everyone about us. You earthlings will say anything to get on TV."

Another alien fiddles with its necklace and chimes in. "But we must know how you made Saucer Forty-three crash. We'll give your memories back to you. Then you can tell us."

"Huh?" you ask. The aliens have your memories?

"We recovered these memory helmets from the crash site," the first alien explains. He holds out two helmets that have wires and spikes sticking from them.

"They contain your memories," he announces. "But after we return them to you, you have to explain how you crashed our saucer. Then we'll let you go. Is it a deal?"

Max glances at you. Should you make a deal with the aliens? And risk putting on one of those weird helmets?

Can you trust them?

To make a deal, turn to PAGE 104.
To say no, go to PAGE 117.

"Okay," you agree. "Let's wait until we turn into werewolves. Then we'll get those hunters!"

You feel sort of bad about biting all those people. But the thrill of the hunt is already growing inside you.

You and Max stay with your wolf pack in the woods until night falls. When the full moon rises, it burns your eyes. You remember your nightmare again.

"It's like that wheel of fire in our dream!" you shout.

"You're right," Max agrees. His voice is already getting husky. Fur is sprouting from you both, and your teeth are getting huge. Your noses are becoming long snouts.

Whoa! You and Max are turning into wolves!

Soon the transformation is complete. You lead your wolf pack toward the abandoned house. Your keen sense of smell tells you that a large group of humans is gathering there.

You creep up to the hunters' camp. You sniff the air. There are dozens of them! Are there too many to attack all at once?

Should you try to get them a few at a time? Or go in with your whole wolf pack all at once?

To try to get the hunters a few at a time, turn to *PAGE 29.*

To attack with your whole pack at once, turn to *PAGE 134.*

You both stare at the little necklace. What *is* it?

"*Zzizna practo,*" it sputters.

"Look at those little buttons," Max exclaims. You see what he means. You press one of the buttons at random.

"*Zzizna* — Saucer Forty-three has crashed," the tiny voice from the necklace announces.

Whoa! Suddenly, you can understand what the voice is saying. Somehow, you changed the voice to English!

"The prisoners have escaped," the voice says.

"Prisoners?" Max gasps.

Another voice pops onto the walkie-talkie. "Don't worry. The robot is closing in on the two prisoners now."

You hear a sound above you and look up. A head peers at you through the bedroom window.

"Yikes!" you shout. It's shiny metal, like a robot head.

Then something *really* weird happens. . . .

The head bobs up. It has no body!

And then it floats out the window!

Head to PAGE 69.

The hunters step out of the shadows around you.

There are at least a dozen of them. They're armed with silver knives, rifles, bows and arrows, even a silver boomerang!

You're doomed!

"Uh..." Max stammers. "We're not werewolves anymore!"

"Yeah, right!" one of the hunters scoffs. "I suppose you've retired!"

The hunters move toward you threateningly. You can't see any way to escape!

What should you do?

You could run for it. Who knows? Maybe the moon will rise soon. Or you could just give yourselves up.

Run? Or surrender?

To try to escape, run to PAGE 51.
To give yourself up, surrender on PAGE 116.

The men advance on you and Max.

"Um . . . can't we talk this over?" you stammer.

"Yeah," Max chimes in. "We don't even know what's going on!"

"You know too much," the man snaps. "Or you wouldn't be sniffing around this base!"

Suddenly, a siren sounds in the distance. You spot something moving behind the men in black suits.

All right! It's a truck full of soldiers headed this way!

"Over here!" you shout to them.

"Grab them! Now!" the man orders.

Two of the men reach for you, but you and Max hold them off with a flurry of punchs. The siren grows closer and closer. After a few moments, the men retreat to their car and peel back toward the gate.

The truck full of soldiers pulls up. You're saved!

But when the soldiers get out, they surround you and Max. "You are under arrest!" one shouts.

Oh, great, you think. Isn't *anyone* on your side?

But then a woman in a lab coat jumps out of the truck.

"Wait a minute!" she shouts. "It's them!"

Turn to PAGE 28.

"Let's just get out of here!" you cry. "We've got to figure out who we are! And we can't find out anything up here."

"Okay, okay," Max whispers. "Just keep quiet."

You press your ear to the attic trapdoor.

"I can't hear anyone down there," you announce.

You push the door open slowly. The ladder unfolds and you put a foot onto it carefully.

You creep down the ladder. A scuffling noise makes you jump.

It sounds like the two dogs.

"It's coming from that direction," Max whispers, pointing down the back stairs. "They must be in the backyard!"

"We'll have to go out the front door," you say.

You creep down the hall. The closed doors in the hallway loom around you. You imagine the woman jumping out and shooting a silver-tipped arrow into your heart.

Gulp.

Then, your nose wrinkles. What's *that*?

"Do you smell something funny?" Max asks.

You try to answer, but the smell is making you gag!

You and Max are surrounded by a cloud of gas!

Turn to PAGE 64.

Max inspects the device closely.

"Hmmm," he mutters. "It has *two* buttons on it. And they've got teeny little labels!"

"What do they say?" you ask.

Max squints at the device.

"One is labeled PARA," Max announces. "The other one says EMER."

"That's a lot of help!" you complain. "PARA could mean *parachute*, or *parallel....*"

"Or para*noid*!" Max snorts. "And who knows *what* EMER means."

"Well, let's try one and see what it does," you suggest.

"Okay," Max agrees. "But which one?"

To try the PARA button, give it a test on PAGE 135.

To try the EMER button, take a shot on PAGE 60.

You thrust out your hand with three fingers showing.

Max has two fingers showing. . . .

"Two plus three is five . . . odd!" Max cries in dismay. "Uh, this was best of three tries, right?"

You snort. "I don't think so. *You're* the bait."

Max gulps. "Just make sure you don't miss with that pile of junk."

Max opens the trapdoor and steals down the ladder. He closes it behind him, leaving it open just a crack so you can see through. He lies on the floor and grabs his ankle.

"Ohhh!" he moans. "I can't run anymore!"

He peers around, listening. There isn't a sound.

"Whoa! I'm in horrible pain!" he screams.

"You're not winning any Oscars for this one," you whisper through the crack.

"*Shhh!*" he hisses.

You start to retort. Then you hear footsteps stomping up the stairs.

"It's the hunter!" Max whispers.

Get ready to spring on PAGE 105.

The door opens on a large, dusty bedroom. The early morning sun is streaming through a window. You blink in the sunlight.

Max closes the door behind him quietly, and presses his ear to it. He shakes his head. Still no sound from downstairs.

An ancient bed stands in the middle of the room. The mattress is ripped to pieces, as if someone hacked it with a knife. Cobwebs cover everything.

"Does any of this look familiar to you?" Max whispers.

You peer intently around the room, hoping something will fall into place. But you've never seen any of this stuff before in your life.

Think harder! You must remember *something*.

You shake your head. "Sorry. Nothing rings a bell."

"Well," he answers, peering out the window. "Wait till you see *this*."

Peer at PAGE 100.

Feathers sprout from your skin. Your arms turn into wings. Your clothes slip from you as you shrink down to the size of a bird.

Cool!

"Brawk!" Max announces from the other cage.

You see what he means. You're small enough to fit between the bars now! This cage could easily hold a wolf, but not a hawk. . . .

Not one of the hunters is watching. They're still celebrating having captured the world's toughest pair of werewolves.

You and Max slip quietly through the bars. You singe your feathers a little when they brush the silver bars.

But who cares? You're free!

You flap your wings and leap from the truck. Now you and Max are the world's toughest pair of were-hawks!

After all, birds of a feather stick together!

THE END

"Good afternoon," the man says.

"What do you want?" the guard asks.

"I'm just here to pick up my two friends!" the man declares, smiling at you and Max.

"Watch out!" Max cries. "That guy's a bad —"

But Max's warning comes too late. The man reaches from the car and grabs the guard by the collar.

"Ack!" the guard yelps. "Let go!"

What should you do?

You could use the guard's phone and call for help. Or just take advantage of the diversion and bolt through the gate.

What'll it be?

To use the guard's phone, turn to PAGE 94.
To run through the gate, turn to PAGE 70.

You decide to let the werewolf hunter cure you. Being a werewolf might be cool — in a sick kind of way. But it's also very scary. And waking up with no memory is one long nightmare.

Thanks, you think at the wolf. *But we don't need any help.*

The wolf obeys your command, bounding away.

"What are you doing?" Max demands.

"I don't want to be a werewolf anymore!" you explain.

The dolls keep up their dance. Now the woman is sprinkling you with herbs and potions. Max looks furious, but the little dolls keep him in line.

The ritual takes the rest of the day. When it finally ends, it's getting dark outside. The dolls collapse around you and Max, lifeless again.

"The moon is still full tonight," the magic woman announces. "Let's see if my sorcery worked."

You step outside. The full moon is rising in the east.

Wow! The moon is like a wheel of fire, you realize. Just like in your dream.

But then you feel a strange sensation. You're growing fur!

Oh, no! The spell didn't work. You're still a werewolf!

Turn to PAGE 61.

You decide to make the saucer crash. No one's stealing your memories twice in one day! You yank the helmet off.

"Why are you doing that?" an alien snaps.

"I can't think with this thing on," you reply, thinking fast. "Just let me take a look at the control panel," you suggest. "Then I can figure out what I did."

The aliens step aside, letting you near a panel at the front of the saucer. It's covered with buttons and levers.

"Just don't touch anything," an alien warns.

You lean over the panel, trying to remember what happened.

There it is! you realize. A big orange button marked with alien writing. That's the one you pushed.

"Let me see," you mutter. "I think I pushed . . . *that* one!"

As you say the words, you stab the button with a finger.

"Get ready to crash!" you shout to Max. You brace yourself.

Turn to PAGE 8.

"Run for it!" you command. You can outrun a bunch of dogs, right?

You crash through the ring of menacing dogs. You hear Max panting behind you. You pound your way toward the trees in the distance. Maybe you can climb one to escape the dogs.

The little dolls scream behind you. The high-pitched sound sends chills up your spine.

Suddenly, a dog cuts in front of you. The little doll riding it turns, screeches . . .

. . . and jumps right at you!

It clutches your leg, its long arms wrapped around you.

"Get off me!" you yell. You kick at the doll as you run.

You watch in horror as it opens its mouth to reveal a row of shiny silver teeth.

Uh-oh, it's going to . . .

"Owwww!" you yell.

Sink your teeth into PAGE 59.

As you ride in the truck, the woman explains everything. Her name is Dr. Sloper, and you and Max have worked with her for two years!

You and Max are secret agents. You were enrolled in the Young Spy Agency when you were two years old. By now, you're experts.

"No wonder we've got such great reflexes!" Max cries.

Dr. Sloper has been working on a new device, called a Matter Slammer. It's supposed to slam you right through the fabric of space. You can travel miles in less than a second!

But the device isn't very accurate yet. You can't control where it will send you. Dr. Sloper put you and Max through it, knowing you could find your way back to the spy base. But somehow, your memories were erased!

"So who were those guys who tried to capture us?" you ask, remembering the two men in black suits.

"They must have been enemy agents," Dr. Sloper guesses. "We must have an enemy spy somewhere on the base!"

"So how do we get our memories back?" Max asks.

"I think your memories may be stored in the machine," Dr. Sloper says. "To get them back, I'll have to slam you again!"

Oh, no! you think. Here we go again!

Turn to PAGE 101.

You decide to shoot at the saucer. No one's going to take you prisoner!

You hoist the zapper, aiming it straight at the saucer.

The saucer tilts toward you, its spinning red lights dazzling your eyes.

It looks as if they've seen you.

Time to open fire!

But as your finger moves toward the firing buttons, you remember that there are *two* of them. You used the blue button last time. That blue ray did a pretty good job on the floating robot head.

But what does the red one do? you wonder. Your finger starts to itch. Should you risk pressing a different button?

Or should you stick with good old blue?

"Shoot!" Max pleads.

Think fast. That saucer's getting closer and closer. . . .

To press the red button, shoot for PAGE 35.
To stick with the blue button, go for PAGE 43.

You jump into the sentry box and grab the phone.

"Help!" you shout.

"Report your situation," a calm voice orders.

"There's a guy here in a car and he's trying to —" you begin, but a hand clamps over your mouth.

"*Mmmmmph!*" you scream into the phone.

But the phone is lifted from your hand by a black-gloved hand. You struggle, but you can't break free of his iron grip.

The man puts the phone to his lips.

"Sorry, wrong number," he announces, and hangs up.

Then he pushes a little box against your arm.

ZZZAAPPP!

And that's the last thing you remember for a while. . . .

Wake up on PAGE 67.

A woman tumbles through the door, crashing to a halt at the bottom of the stairs. She pulls out a bow and arrow and scans the room. You hunch down lower, hoping she doesn't see you.

What a weirdo! you think.

All sorts of strange stuff hangs from her belt. A pair of scary-looking dolls are tied to her back. Their shiny teeth give you the creeps.

Who is she? you wonder. And what is she looking for?

Two big dogs follow her into the house. The woman holds a piece of cloth out to them. They smell it and start to growl.

"Find them!" she orders.

The dogs sniff the floor around them. You and Max nervously pull back from the stairs.

Then Max points wordlessly at your shirt. You glance down. There's a big piece ripped out of it. And it's the same color as the piece of cloth in the woman's hand. . . .

She's hunting for *you*!

Turn to PAGE 46.

Suddenly, Max explodes into action! He stomps the foot of the man holding him.

"Ow!" the man howls, dropping Max to the floor.

Max delivers a flurry of blows to the stomach. The man stumbles back.

"Hey!" the other man yells. You feel his hold on you lessen for a moment.

In a fraction of a second, you find yourself following Max's lead. You flex your muscles and burst from the man's grip. With one karate chop to the neck, you knock him out.

Max's opponent also falls to the floor, out stone cold.

You and Max find yourselves gawking at the two unconscious men.

"Whoa!" you exclaim. "Who taught you how to do that?"

"I don't know," Max stammers. "Who taught *you* how to do *that?*"

You search your mind for the answer.

"I have no idea!" you admit.

But whoever it was, you owe them a favor. . . .

Turn to PAGE 45.

Max throws open the attic door, and an avalanche of junk falls out. The first piece hits the hunter right on the head!

"All riii —" you start to shout.

But the hunter's fingers slip from the silver-tipped arrow. And it flies straight for you!

THWACK!

"Ahhh!" you cry. The arrow pins you to the wall.

You thrash and claw at the arrow, but it burns your hands. Suddenly, you feel yourself changing. Fur sprouts from your arms and face. Your hands turn into claws!

Max jumps down onto the pile of stuff covering the hunter.

"Whoa!" he exclaims. "You're a . . . werewolf."

"Ahhh!" you roar. "It burns! It burns!"

"I must be a werewolf too!" he cries. "That's why we can't remember anything. It must have been a full moon last night."

I'm a werewolf! you think as your vision dims.

Correction — you *were* a werewolf.

Because that arrow had a silver tip. And that makes this . . .

THE END.

"You're right! Let's stay hidden," you decide. "This is all too weird!"

You glance around quickly. There's a door at the other end of the hallway.

You point at the door. "We can hide in there."

Max frowns.

"Why don't we get a look at whoever is downstairs?" he suggests. "We can sneak to the top of the stairs and peek down."

You gulp. What if they see you? Your instincts are telling you that you should hide.

The banging sound comes again.

What are you going to do? Hide in the room down the hall? Or take a peek?

Think fast!

To hide down the hall, turn to PAGE 63.

To sneak to the stairs and take a look, creep to PAGE 27.

"Ahhhhhh!" you scream as you wake up.

Whoa! you think, shaking your head. That was some nightmare. Your head is spinning like a top.

Images from the dream dance in your mind. Dozens of werewolves hunting and howling all night long.

You also remember a huge spinning wheel of fire. And some really scary little dolls.

What a weird dream!

At least it's over. You're glad to be back in your nice warm bed, that's for sure.

Wait a minute. This isn't your nice warm bed! What's going on? You're on the floor, in some dusty old room.

And boy, is it crowded in here!

THE END

100

You stare out the window.

What *is* that?

A flaming wreck is scattered all over the field behind the house. Twisted bits of metal lie sparkling in the grass. A deep crater shows where something hit the ground hard.

What could it be? you wonder. Some kind of airplane crash?

You peer closer, and your heart begins to pound. There are bodies in the wreck! They're dressed in silvery suits. They're tiny. Only about two feet tall.

"Like in the dream!" Max whispers. You nod, remembering the little figures in your nightmare.

"Was that dream . . . real?" you ask.

Then you both hear something behind you. It sounds like huge feet pounding the old boards of the house.

Someone is clomping up the stairs!

Someone big . . .

Clomp your way to PAGE 115.

"No way!" Max protests. "I've had enough brain damage for one day!"

"But it's the only way to restore your memories!" Dr. Sloper argues. "The machine has an exact recording of your brain when you were slammed."

You arrive at the base. Inside, you gaze at the Matter Slammer. It has a huge, round platform, with lights blinking all around its edge.

Whoa! you think. It's like the spinning wheel of fire in your dream!

"What if the memory loss wasn't an accident?" Max suggests.

"What do you mean?" Dr. Sloper asks.

"What if an enemy spy programmed the Slammer to erase our memories," he explains. "And ordered those guys in black suits to go get us."

You gulp. If the machine's been messed with, you shouldn't use it again. But your memories are stored inside it.

Should you use the machine? Or look for an enemy spy first?

To use the machine again, slam to PAGE 47.
To look for an enemy agent, turn to PAGE 108.

Your vision is starting to blur.

"Whazz happening?" you croak. Your words slur in your mouth.

The woman steps out of the shadows. A doll leers at you from her back. It's carrying a tiny bow and arrow.

"Just a little wolfbane to calm you down," she explains.

"Wolfbane?" Max manages to murmur.

Your knees buckle and you fall. Max staggers a few steps and then tumbles to the floor.

"It's great stuff for capturing werewolves," the woman announces.

Werewolves again! She must be crazy! you think.

But that's the last thing you think, for a while. . . .

Wake up on PAGE 53.

Soon Max spots a river in the distance. It looks just like the one on the map. You follow the river for a few twists and turns to make sure.

Then you see a big bridge not far away.

"That's on the map too!" Max exclaims. "We know exactly where we are!"

"Too bad we don't know *who* we are," you add glumly.

You cross the bridge. You're headed straight for the Slammer Project headquarters, whatever that is. It's slow-going, tramping across the fields. But at least you're getting closer.

"We should be there in another few minutes," Max announces.

"I'm not so sure," you say, pointing ahead.

A high, barbed-wire fence is right in your path. It stretches in both directions as far as you can see.

And when you read the sign on it, your jaw drops.

TOP SECRET INSTALLATION
KEEP OUT!!!
DEADLY FORCE AUTHORIZED

Head to PAGE 131.

"Okay," you announce. "Just give us back our memories!"

The alien thrusts the helmets toward you.

"Put them on!" he orders.

You and Max exchange nervous looks and obey.

Your helmet fits snugly. It starts to hum, then shake.

It's doing something to your brain!

And then you start to remember everything. . . .

You were playing in your backyard with Max. Hey, his name really *is* Max! He's your best friend. Suddenly, a saucer appeared over your heads. The aliens took the two of you aboard. They made you take a bunch of tests. It wasn't so bad, sort of like playing video games. But then they told you they had to erase your memories. You'd been captured by aliens, the neatest thing *ever*, and you weren't going to remember it!

No way!

Those aliens put a helmet on you, just like the one you're wearing now. But as they turned it on, you jumped for the controls of the craft. You didn't want to forget the coolest thing that had ever happened to you!

The saucer began to twist and screech, just like the wheel of fire in your dream.

Turn to PAGE 38.

Keep quiet. Keep quiet! you order yourself. Your sweaty hands grasp a chair at the base of the junk pile.

The hunter steps into view below. But she's not under the trapdoor.

Not yet!

"So, I've finally caught you!" she taunts Max.

"But why are you chasing us?" he asks.

"You have an awful disease," she announces. "It makes you do terrible things that you can't remember."

You strain to hear her through the crack in the door. Could she be telling the truth?

She takes a step forward. She's right under you!

Your hands start to shake.

"But I can cure you!" she proclaims.

"Now!" Max shouts.

But what if you really *do* have some terrible disease? What if that's why you can't remember who you are?

Should you spring the trap? Or give up and ask for her help?

She's glancing up! You only have one second to decide. . . .

To spring the trap, go to PAGE 39.
To give yourself up, turn to PAGE 119.

You decide to give up.

Maybe you'll get the answers you're looking for. And you didn't really want to get bopped on the head with that club.

The soldier's radio pops to life. *"Come in, Unit Five."*

The soldier calmly gives his position.

Before long, a truck full of soldiers arrives. They jump out and surround you.

Max glances at you nervously, his hands high in the air.

You're definitely caught now.

A tall woman in a lab coat jumps out of the truck. She dashes forward, waving at the soldiers.

"Wait!" she shouts. "It's them!"

"Whoa!" Max exclaims. "She knows who we are!"

Turn to PAGE 28.

"No way!" you shout. "I don't believe you."

You stagger to your feet. You've got to get away from this crazy woman. You step toward the edge of the circle.

Suddenly, one of the dolls comes to life! It reaches out its long arms and grabs your legs.

The doll's silver teeth chomp into your leg!

"Ahhh!" you scream. Your leg feels as if it's on fire.

You leap back toward the center of the circle. The doll lets go. You stare at it in horror.

The woman laughs. "My dolls are too powerful, werewolf!"

You gulp, rubbing your leg. Wow! Silver burns you. Silver is supposed to burn werewolves. Maybe you *are* a werewolf!

"Now I'll begin the cure," the woman announces. She starts a weird chant. One by one, the rest of the dolls come horribly to life. They begin a jerky dance, moving like puppets on strings. Their silver teeth glimmer cruelly.

Max nudges you. You tear your eyes from the horrifying dolls and follow his glance.

Out the window, you see a face watching you through the window.

Whoa! It's a wolf!

Shall I help you, Master? it asks.

Turn to PAGE 113.

"I think we should find out if there's an enemy agent first!" you decide.

"But you need your memories back," Dr. Sloper insists.

"We've been okay without them so far," Max declares.

"Let's start by checking out the Slammer," you order.

You and Max inspect the machine. You open a long panel along its base. You don't understand anything about the circuits and wires inside the device, but you've learned to trust your instincts.

"Hey, look at this!" Max exclaims, pointing.

You peer closely into the machine. A bunch of chips on a circuit board have been deliberately smashed.

"Someone has been messing around here!" you announce.

"Let's see if we can find some fingerprints!" Max suggests.

"That won't be necessary!" Dr. Sloper interrupts.

You and Max turn around.

Dr. Sloper has some sort of weird device pointed at you! She squeezes it, and a bolt of light shoots toward your feet.

"Yeeow!" you both shout, leaping into the air. That stung!

"Hands up!" she commands.

Turn to PAGE 65.

The wolves surround you and Max.

"Aren't you guys on our side?" Max pleads.

"I mean, we're werewolves," you chime in. "At least, we *think* we are. . . ."

The biggest wolf in the pack trots up to you and sniffs your hand. You shake with fear.

Don't bite me! you think.

We would never bite you, Master, the wolf thinks. *We are here to serve you both!*

"Cool!" you shout. "Somehow, we can hear the wolf's thoughts!"

You and Max *must* be werewolves.

"Whoa!" Max exclaims. "We're the bosses of a wolf pack."

But there is much danger here, the wolf thinks at you.

"Wh-wh-what do you mean?" you stammer. You've had enough danger for one day.

More hunters are coming, the wolf leader explains. *Dozens of them!*

Hunt for PAGE 130.

You decide to keep your deal with the aliens.

You peer at the alien's control panel. "I think I pressed that orange button there."

"Aha!" an alien exclaims. "The flight stabilizer override. We'll have to put a lock on that button."

Another alien pats you on the back. "Thanks for your help. It's too bad we have to erase your memories again."

No! you think. There must be some way you can remember what happened today. You wrack your brain.

But there's no way out of it. You hang your head, shoving your hands into your pockets.

Something in your left pocket jabs one of your fingers.

Hey! Is that what you think it is? A pencil.

It gives you a pretty good idea.

"Before you do erase my memory," you ask, "do you think I could, you know, use the bathroom?"

An alien nods. "Yes, we have human-style facilities on board."

"Perfect," you exclaim. "I'll just be a minute."

A few minutes later, the aliens use the memory helmet on you. But you have a strange little smile on your face. . . .

Turn to PAGE 25.

"It *is*?" you cry.

Your heart drops. Your memories must be TO-TALLY erased. You don't even remember what you look like!

And what is the Young Spy Agency?

"Let's show this to those guys downstairs," Max suggests. "Maybe they can tell us something."

You head downstairs. But there's no one there.

Oh, no! The men are gone.

"They escaped!" Max yelps.

"They can't have gotten far," you shout.

"Not far at all," comes a voice from behind you.

WHOMP! A blinding blow lands on the back of your skull.

Your reflexes kick into action. You spin around, but another blow sends you to the ground.

Then everything goes dark. . . .

Wake up on PAGE 67.

You and Max decide to let them go. After all, if you're dangerous lunatics, you need to get back to the hospital.

You carefully untie them.

"Sorry about beating you up and everything," Max apologizes.

"We just didn't know what was going on," you explain.

"Don't worry about it," one of them laughs.

"After all, you just made our job a lot easier," the other adds. He pulls a little box from his pocket. Is it a phone?

"Yeah," the first one agrees. "Usually it's a lot harder than this to catch secret agents."

"Secret agents!" you shout.

But like lightning, the man presses the little box to your arm and pushes a button.

ZAP!

And suddenly, everything goes dark.

Zap your way to PAGE 67.

What? you think.

I asked if I should help you escape, Master, the wolf repeats.

Wow! Somehow the wolf is sending its thoughts to you. And it can read your thoughts too!

You *must* be a werewolf!

You try to think clearly. Should you order the wolf to rescue you? You definitely want to escape these weirdo dolls!

But if you go with the wolf, you'll stay a werewolf. The woman says she can cure you. That way you won't forget everything once a month!

What should you do? Order the wolf to save you? Or let the werewolf hunter work her magic?

To tell the wolf to save you, turn to PAGE 24.
To let the woman cure you, turn to PAGE 89.

"A Matter Slammer!" you realize.

A huge circular platform almost fills the room. Around its edge are blinking lights. This is the wheel of fire from your nightmare!

"In here!" a muffled voice shouts. Oh, no! They found you!

"There's only one way to escape!" Max shouts. "We have to use the machine!"

"But we'll get mixed into a horrible monster," you protest.

"We'll go one at a time," Max orders. "And I call *first*!"

He jumps on the platform. You leap to the controls. You recognize the SLAM button. You push it.

The lights on the platform start to spin. A screeching noise fills the room. Then Max disappears!

He escaped! But someone's starting to bang on the door. You better get going!

You push the SLAM button again. As the lights start to spin, you jump onto the platform.

The door bursts open! Men in black suits are everywhere, but they're too afraid to go near the device.

But running through their legs is a blur of scales and fur.

Hiiisswoof! it yowls as it jumps at you.

"Nooooooo!" you scream.

Scream your way to PAGE 56.

"Run!" Max whispers.

You nod frantically. Whatever is coming, you don't want to meet it until you know for sure what's going on.

Max steps toward the door but freezes. The footsteps sound like they're coming right toward your hiding place!

You're trapped!

You both peer frantically around the room. The only place to hide is under the bed.

But then Max motions toward the window. You grimace at the thought of climbing out. What if you fall?

What's it going to be? Under the bed? Or out the window?

Think fast . . .

To hide under the bed, crawl to PAGE 21.
To climb out the window, jump to PAGE 48.

116

"We surrender!" you shout, throwing up your hands.

"Yeah, don't shoot!" Max chimes in.

They close in and take you prisoner, tying your hands. They march you back to the house. The hunters' Jeeps and cars are parked all around it.

Inside a big truck are two huge cages.

You gulp when you see them.

Silver bars! You'll *never* escape.

They shove you and Max into the cages.

"We'll sell them to the zoo!" one suggests.

"Nah," another hunter disagrees. "Let's do some scientific experiments! We can find out how this werewolf stuff works."

They laugh and joke, ignoring you and Max. You feel miserable. Maybe you should have run for it.

"Hey, look!" Max whispers. You follow his gaze.

Across the field, the sun is setting.

Soon it's dark. The moon rises. It's still pretty full. And as you stare at it, you remember the wheel of fire in your dream. The moon looks just like it!

"Brawk!" you squawk.

Flap your way to PAGE 87.

"No deal!" you exclaim. You don't trust these kidnapping aliens and their weird helmet.

"I agree," Max chimes in.

"You have made us very unhappy," an alien snaps. "First, you destroy one of our saucers. And now you won't help us prevent it from happening again."

"We'll have to repay you with something very special," another alien threatens.

Uh-oh. It looks like you *really* made them mad this time.

"Wh-wh-what are you going to do to us?" Max stammers.

The alien laughs. "We're going to let you go."

"Let us go?" you repeat in disbelief.

"*After* a little session with a programming device," the alien finishes. He pulls out another helmet, covered with mean-looking spikes. It's even scarier than the memory helmet!

Two aliens grab your arms.

"Noooo!" you scream.

But he puts the helmet on your head. It makes your brain feel *very* strange. . . .

Program your way to PAGE 127.

118

Yikes! You can't take your eyes off the ugly creature. It has the face, legs, and tail of a dog, but with a long, scaly body.

"Look at this poor thing," the man continues, stroking the weird animal. "When we try to slam two creatures at once, they wind up mixed together!"

Grrrriiissss! the dog-snake complains. You flinch at the horrible sound.

The man laughs at your discomfort. "We think we've got the problem solved. But we need to test it with two humans."

"T-t-two humans?" Max stammers.

"No way!" you shout, straining against the handcuffs.

You don't want to be transformed into some half-you, half-Max monster!

But what can you do with handcuffs on? Should you jump at the man right now, trying to take him by surprise? Or play along for a while and wait for a better chance to escape?

Think carefully. After all, you don't want to get *mixed up*, do you?

To try to escape now, turn to **PAGE 74**.
To play along for a while, turn to **PAGE 42**.

"Wait!" you cry. "I give up."

"What are you doing?" shrieks Max.

You push open the attic door. As the ladder unfolds, it strikes the hunter on the head. She's knocked back, but she whirls around with her bow in hand.

It's aimed right at your chest. You drop to your hands and knees.

She fires!

Whoops! Your hands slip. You're falling down the ladder!

The arrow whizzes past you. You skid down the ladder and hit the floor painfully.

The arrow lands with a *THWACK* in the middle of the tower of junk. The pile sways with the impact. It's right above your head.

"Uh-oh!" you croak. You try to move, but pain shoots through your body.

You stare up with horror.

The junk pile is starting to fall!

Pile onto PAGE 36.

"Get on the platform!" Dr. Sloper orders.

The lights around the platform are starting to spin. It's just like the wheel of fire in your nightmare!

Only, this time it'll be one of those *falling* dreams.

You step onto the platform. The spinning lights make your head spin. You gaze at Dr. Sloper and realize that she is staring at the lights too. For a moment, she looks a little bit dizzy. . . .

Without thinking, you leap into action!

You throw yourself from the platform at Dr. Sloper. She raises the device, but you knock it away.

She punches you in the stomach as you fly past. *OOOF!* You crumple to the ground.

Max jumps at her. But she throws him over her head with a crash.

Whoa! you think. Dr. Sloper is even a better secret agent than you and Max! She totally fooled you.

And she's a better fighter.

Dr. Sloper calmly walks over to where the weapon landed and picks it up. You're doomed!

But then you see where she's standing. . . .

Take a look on PAGE 17.

You and Max decide to cure yourselves. Maybe being a regular kid won't be so bad.

The book lists a bunch of herbs you need to perform the magic. Fortunately, because you're werewolves you've got a great sense of smell. You sniff out everything you need and get started.

"Now when those werewolf hunters come, we can just say, 'What werewolves?'" Max jokes.

"Or, 'Where werewolves?'" you answer.

"Ugh," he responds, holding his nose at your joke.

Max gets a fire going, and you throw the herbs in.

You're just about to start reading the magic words that will cure you, when you hear a sound behind you.

Werewolf hunters?

You spin around, imagining a silver arrow flying into your heart.

But you see something completely different.

A pack of wolves!

Turn to PAGE 68.

"Let's climb it!" you insist. You're sure that your incredible reflexes will kick in once you're halfway up.

You leap into the lower branches of the tree. You easily make your way up to the top.

You were right! With your amazing abilities, this is going to be a piece of cake.

The branch that stretches over the fence takes your weight easily. You creep out farther and farther. The metal spikes of the barbed wire gleam in the sun.

Don't get nervous! you order yourself.

Suddenly, a branch under one of your hands starts writhing! You pull back with a start.

Yikes! It's a snake!

You cling to the tree with your other hand. The tree-snake glares up at you with cold black eyes. It opens its mouth to reveal huge fangs.

Hisssssssss!

Uh-oh! This tree's bite is worse than its bark!

Turn to lucky PAGE 13.

Taking careful aim, you press the blue button. *ZAAAAAP!*

A bright blue ray of light leaps from the end of the zapper. The metal head explodes into a shower of sparks.

You got it!

"Good shot!" Max shouts.

You laugh with relief, dropping the zapper and leaning back into the grass. Suddenly, the little necklace starts to talk again.

"One of the escaped prisoners has destroyed the robot!" a voice exclaims.

"We must recapture the prisoners ourselves," another answers.

"Uh-oh!" Max cries. "Do you think they're . . . ?"

You nod your head.

They're talking about *you!*

Turn to PAGE 55.

The wolves are closing in on you!

"What's wrong?" you shout. "I thought you wanted to serve us!"

As the last remains of your werewolf nature fade away, you can barely hear the leader's thoughts.

You're not werewolves anymore, but we'll still serve you, it thinks, growling. *For dinner!*

Uh-oh.

This is going to be one dinner you wish you'd skipped.

Because you have a terrible feeling that they're going to *wolf* down their food. . . .

THE END

You hand the zapper to Max and grab the helmet on the left.

"I hope those are *your* memories," Max says nervously.

"Me too!" you agree.

As soon as the helmet is on your head, it starts to hum. A deafening buzzing noise fills your head.

Uh-oh. Is something going wrong?

But then the memories come flooding back.

You were playing with your best friend, Max. Hey, his name really *is* Max! Then a flying saucer appeared — and took you on board!

The aliens tested you with all kinds of weird machines. You were pretty scared. Then they told you they had to erase your memories. No way would they let you remember you'd been captured by aliens!

So as they put the memory helmet on you, you grabbed the controls of the saucer. You made it crash!

But not before your memories had been erased.

"Whoa!" you exclaim, pulling off the helmet. "No one's ever going to believe this!"

"Don't worry about that," Max snorts. "I have a feeling that *everyone's* going to believe us. . . ."

Turn to PAGE 54.

"I say we tie them up," you announce. "They *must* know what's going on."

"Okay," Max reluctantly agrees.

You find some old rope and tie the men's hands behind their backs. Soon they start to stir.

One snaps his eyes open and struggles with the cords.

"Let me go!" he shouts.

"Not until you tell us what's going on," you demand.

"Who are we? That might be a good place to start," Max suggests.

"Hah!" the man snorts. "So the mind-wipe worked pretty well, didn't it?"

"Mind-wipe?" you ask.

"That's what it's called," he explains. "It's a machine that makes you forget everything about yourself. Your name. Your past. *Everything.*"

Your jaw drops. Why would someone do that to you?

"No way!" Max blurts. "Who would do that to us?"

"The doctors at the mental hospital," the man explains. "You two are the most dangerous people in the world!"

"You're crazy!" you object.

But maybe, just maybe, *you're* the one who's crazy. . . .

Turn to PAGE 72.

A few hours later, the saucer passes over your house.

The aliens let you out, and you wave happily back to them. Those aliens are great. They even let you keep your memories!

You're glad to be home. Your parents must be worried. You're going to be in trouble after disappearing for almost two whole days.

But your parents won't be mad for long. You've got a little present for them. You glance happily at the programming helmet under your arm. Once your parents put it on, they won't be mad at you at all.

They'll be happy, just like you are.

Happy to serve the aliens!

The aliens need servants. Earth people who'll do exactly what they're told. One session with the programming helmet, and you're a happy servant for the rest of your life!

Which makes this a very happy

END.

The hunters' feet thud up to where you're lying.

"We got them both!" they shout. "Hurray!"

One of the hunters reaches down to check your wound.

"Hah!" He laughs. "*I* got this one. And you all laughed at my silver boomerang."

You see his hand a few inches in front of you. With your last drop of strength, you reach out and nip his finger with your teeth.

"Ouch!" he complains.

Yes! You bit him!

Now *he's* a were-hawk.

You lie back and smile. You may be a goner, but you've gotten your revenge. When the full moon comes, that hunter's going to be awfully surprised. . . .

THE END

Before you can react, Max jumps up and grabs the alien.

"Nobody move, or my friend shoots him!" he yells.

Catching on, you wave the zapper. "I'll do it!"

"Wait, don't shoot!" the other aliens anxiously shout.

"What do you want?" the captive alien asks. "We'll give you anything! Just don't hurt me."

"Tell us what happened," Max orders. "Why can't we remember anything?"

"One of our saucers captured you," the captive alien explains. "We mean no harm. We just like to test earthlings."

You gulp. You were captured by aliens!

"We erased your memories so that you wouldn't tell anyone," the alien adds. "But you went crazy and damaged the saucer."

"It crashed!" another alien cries. "Only you two survived."

"Give us our memories back!" you demand.

"All right," the alien agrees. "But we have to find the memory helmets that were used on you."

The aliens search the field while you nervously wait with your captive. As you watch the little figures, you can hardly believe this is happening.

Finally, one of the aliens comes back.

"We found them!" he announces. "But we have a problem. . . ."

Turn to PAGE 12.

The wolves explain that you and Max are the world's two most notorious werewolves. You're so famous that the werewolf hunters are gathering to catch you — and destroy you. Tonight.

"It's nice to be wanted," Max mutters.

Your heart pounds as you imagine dozens of hunters after you. It's not fair! What did you ever do to them?

Then you remember that you *do* turn into a bloodthirsty monster every month. Gulp.

"We need a plan!" you proclaim.

"Well, why don't we sneak up on the hunters and bite them?" Max suggests. "We could make *them* werewolves!"

"We'd have to wait for another full moon," you protest.

The wolf leader growls for your attention. *The moon will still be full tonight*, it thinks.

"But do we really want to make more werewolves?" you ask. "Why don't we pretend to be hunters? And find out their plans."

You and Max argue for a while. Should you attack the hunters when you turn into wolves tonight? Or spy on them today while you're still human?

To attack the hunters, turn to PAGE 79.
To spy on them, turn to PAGE 16.

"I-I-I don't like the look of that!" Max stammers.

You gulp. "Are you sure this is the right way?"

Max nods his head.

You spot a tree that overhangs the fence.

"Maybe we could climb that tree and jump over," you suggest.

Max eyes the tree and frowns. "We could just walk along the fence for a while. Maybe there's a gate or something."

You read the threatening sign again.

"I don't think they'll let us in," you conclude. "And if we want to know what's going on, we've got to get in there."

What should you do? Climb the tree to get over the fence? Or try to find another way in?

To climb the tree, turn to PAGE 122.

To look for another way in, turn to PAGE 52.

"Uh-oh!" Max mutters. But it comes out more like a growl.

You gaze at him in horror. Fur is sprouting from his face and arms. And the same thing is happening to you!

The full moon is blazing like a wheel of fire. Just like in your weird nightmare! You're turning into a wolf!

But the nightmare's only beginning. . . .

You turn around. All the hunters are staring at you in disbelief.

"It's them!" someone shouts.

And all the hunters' silver arrows, spears, swords, and other weapons are aimed right at you and Max!

It looks like you outfoxed yourselves.

Or is that, out-wolfed yourselves?

Either way, this is . . .

THE END.

Suddenly, soldiers' start appearing out of nowhere all around you!

They grab the bad guys.

All right! You've been rescued!

"Who are you guys?" you cry.

"Don't you remember?" one asks. "We work at the Slammer Project with you. We're on your side."

You scratch your head. Then you figure it out. They must have used the Slammer to come save you. That's how they just appeared out of thin air.

"But how did you know where we were?" you ask.

"Because you activated your emergency beacon, of course," one of your rescuers explains.

"*Emerg*ency!" Max exclaims.

"Don't you remember calling for help?" the soldier asks.

"That's going to take some explaining," you begin. "You see, we had this terrible nightmare —"

"But fortunately," Max interrupts, "it has a happy ending."

THE END

134

You decide to lead one massive attack. You've had enough sneaking around! You and Max order the pack to surround the hunters' camp.

"*Ahwooo!*" you howl, signaling your wolves to attack.

You charge into the camp, your bared teeth glinting in the moonlight. You search madly for a hunter to attack.

But for some reason, you can't find anyone.

You plunge into one of the tents.

Peeeww! There aren't any hunters here. Just a bunch of smelly old socks. What's going on?

You trot back outside. The other wolves are all milling around in confusion.

You hear the sound of helicopters and look up. A huge net floats down over the entire camp.

Oh, no! It's a trap!

You struggle to escape the net, but it's too sturdy. Laughing hunters appear from the house. They start shooting tranquilizer darts!

THWACK! You feel a sting as a dart sinks into your shoulder.

You howl once more as you fall asleep. . . .

Wake up on PAGE 18.

"Let's try PARA!" you decide. "Maybe it'll call for a bunch of paratroopers!"

Max shrugs and pushes the button.

Immediately, the little device starts to spew out gas!

"Oh, no!" you scream, trying to cover your mouth. But eventually you have to take a breath. . . .

And when you do, you find you can't move. Not at all.

You're *paralyzed!*

The bad guys laugh when they find you unable to move. But a little paralysis doesn't stop the experiment. Soon, you and Max are lying on the Matter Slammer.

Wow! The huge machine looks just like the spinning wheel of fire from your dream.

The lights around its circular edge blink and spin, making you dizzier and dizzier.

You try to scream, but you can't!

You're head is spinning, and spinning. . . .

Turn to PAGE 62.

"What?" Max cries. "Why wouldn't we tell everyone?"

You shake your head. "Because if anyone finds out about this, I won't be able to keep this zapper. I'm going to pull off the biggest bank robbery in history."

"Yeah, right!" Max snorts. "My friend the bank robber!"

"I'm *not* your friend," you snap. And as Max peers into your eyes, he begins to see the truth. You aren't his old friend anymore. You've got new memories now. . . .

"You chose the wrong helmet!" Max shouts. "You don't remember who you really are!"

No. You remember *exactly* who you are. The world's best bank robber. At least, you were — until the aliens captured you and emptied your mind into that helmet.

Now your memories are back, though. So what if they're not in the right body? This little-kid body will do just fine.

After all, nobody would suspect a child of being a bank robber!

From now on, robbing banks is going to be *child's play*!

THE END

"Let's look upstairs," you decide.

You and Max dash up the stairs. There *must* be something up here that can help you remember who you are.

The weird, slanted hallway stretches out before you. It makes you dizzy again.

Concentrate! you order yourself.

You head back to the room where you woke up. Your eyes scan the dusty floor.

"*There's* something," you announce.

You pick up a little rectangle of plastic from the floor. Peering closely at it, you see that it's some sort of ID card. There's a picture of some kid on it. And the words YOUNG SPY AGENCY.

You thrust it out to Max. "Does this ring a bell?"

He gulps, glancing between you and the ID.

"Of course it does," he cries. "That picture is *you!*"

Turn to PAGE 111.

About the Author

R.L. Stine is the most popular author in America. He is the creator of the *Goosebumps, Give Yourself Goosebumps, Fear Street,* and *Ghosts of Fear Street* series, among other popular books. He has written over 250 scary novels for kids. Bob lives in New York City with his wife, Jane, teenage son, Matt, and dog, Nadine.